THE NIRA CHRONICLES

BOOK 1

KORA KNIGHT

ISBN: 9781976872952
Independently published

Edited by Tash Hatzipetrou

Cover art by LAS-T
www.artstation.com/las-t
https://las-t.deviantart.com

Titles available from Kora Knight:

The Nira Chronicles
Kríe Captivity (Book 1)
Zercy (Book 2)

Upending Tad: A Journey of Erotic Discovery
Loser Takes All (Book 1)
Test of Endurance (Book 2)
Sideline Submission (Book 3)
Prized Possession (Book 4)
Bringing It Home (Book 5)
Afterglow (Book 6)

THE DUNGEON BLACK DUOLOGY
(An Upending Tad Spin-off: Max and Sean)
Unearthed (Book 1)
Revived (Book 2)

Anthology
This Beautiful Escape (Volume 2)
The short story, "Closing Time,"
featuring a cameo with Tad and Scott.

For every heart and mind that delights in the wonders of limitless imagination, whose home is Earth, but whose playground lies amidst the stars.

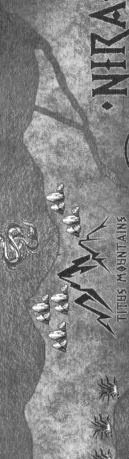

·NIRA·

LAND OF THE TOHRI

TITHS MOUNTAINS

★ Science Team

★ Rescue Team

RIVER PIXEM

MIGHTY REALM OF THE KRIE

CHAPTER ONE

* * *

Astrum Industries Search & Rescue

Location: Planet Nira of the neighboring star system, Siri

"Thirty thousand feet and looking good."

Exiting the stratosphere's dense orange gases, Garret Scott and his co-pilot maneuvered their aircraft into the lower atmosphere. After miles of descent in virtually zero visibility—the high altitude cloud cover having been thick as pea soup—it was reassuring and incredible to finally see what they were heading toward.

"Whoa. Damn. Would you look at that." Kegan scanned the alien planet, awed by its beauty.

A tapestry of rich purples, oranges and blues, intertwined in a backdrop of green. It was stunning. What's more, with nearly the same land to water ratio as Earth, it had an unexpectedly comforting appeal. Like home, but not quite, albeit definitely just as stunning.

Not that Garret missed Earth all that much. He'd left a lot of bullshit behind when he joined the space program. Had been more than happy to get the fuck out of dodge. Too much drama and backstabbing, whether from family members or company politics. Not the kind of excitement he'd been hoping for, making him one bored-off-his-gourd commercial airline pilot. So when he got that call for the search-and-rescue job he'd been gunning for, he'd nearly shit himself.

Goodbye stagnant lifestyle, hello grand adventure.

To be fair, though, being a couple years in, there *were* some things he did kind of miss. Real G. Solid ground. True home-cooked meals. That and sex whenever he wanted it. Up on the space station, or traversing Earth's neighboring star systems, he didn't exactly have much opportunity. Sure, there were just as many girls abroad as guys, but beside the fact that the dudes were better looking—which was saying a lot since he wasn't gay—everyone was just too busy. Had he known that space life would be so demanding, he never would have—Ha! Shit yeah, he fucking would have. Minimal to no sex or not, this was still way better than the doldrums. Besides, he had five fingers that worked perfectly well.

"Twenty thousand feet," Kegan stated absently, eyes shifting back to the view.

Garret stared on, too, as they continued their descent, raptly taking in the new world. Lush and teeming, it exuded not only life, but an exhilarating air of promise. For discovery, and advancements, but most importantly, sentient engagement. No wonder the scientists Garret's team was tasked to locate had wanted to go there so bad. As soon as the company's scouting department had mapped it out as new territory, they'd busted down the doors shouting first dibs for an expedition. And their loud, determined asses had gotten it.

Although, now Garret couldn't help wondering if they wished they hadn't. After all, it'd been a year since the scientists had come there, and nearly just as long since their distress beacon had been picked up. Hell, they'd fallen off the grid damn near the moment they arrived. Unfortunately, the concept of traveling through wormholes was still just that; a concept, a puzzle yet to be solved. So even though Garret's team had been dispatched almost immediately, it'd taken them a good year to get there. Would've been a whole lot longer, though, had their base of operations not relocated to the same star system just before the scientists departed. Either way, even though Garret's spacecraft moved fast, it didn't move *that* fucking fast. But, hey, they were there now, all ready to search and rescue, and that's what ultimately mattered.

Shouldn't be too hard an endeavor, either. They had the scientists' distress beacon blinking clear as day on their scanners. Get in, find their boys, all quick as a snap. Maybe they'd even have some time to sight-see.

Their vessel lurched, then started to shudder.

Kegan frowned and hit the intercom. "Picking up unexpected turbulence, guys. Make sure you're buckled up tight."

The aircraft quaked harder. Garret looked at his co-pilot. "This shit wasn't coming up on the radar."

Kegan shook his head and scanned the controls. "Nah, man. It wasn't. Not sure where it's coming from."

Another vicious shake, then a sharp drop in altitude. Nothing that as pilots they weren't accustomed to, but the intensity of it was still disconcerting.

"Hang tight," Garret shouted over the vibrations. "Lower elevation should help."

But it didn't. Not really. Continued for so long, in fact, that Garret started to worry screws would start shimmying free. Turbulence, after all, wasn't known to take planes down, but malfunctioning equipment was.

The unsettled voices of their teammates in back peeled through the pilots' earpieces.

"What the fuck, guys? You trying to make milkshakes?"

"Goddamn! Please tell us you still got this."

"Yes, we still got this," Garret irritably bit back. "Turbulence is something we just gotta ride out. You boys ain't green. You know how this works."

"Whatever. Just get us to the ground in one piece. Preferably with my organs still intact."

"And my nut sac still outside my fucking body. You got us slamming around so hard back here, they're trying to seek fucking shelter."

Kegan choked back a laugh, even as he warily eyed the wide spread of controls. "T-t-ten thousand f-f-feet," he stammered, teeth clattering hard. "Not seeing an end to this shit."

"Me, n-neither." Garret readied the landing gear. "B-But we're almost at our d-d-destination."

Out of nowhere something big slammed them from underneath.

"Whoa!" Kegan shouted. "What the fuck was that?"

System failure alarms wailed to life.

Garret gaped. "Holy shit. Whatever it was, it just wrecked our right burner."

A massive flying creature flew into view ahead of them. Then another joined it. And another.

Kegan's mouth fell open, eyes going wide. "Good God! What the fuck are *those*?"

Good question. With bodies as big as Clydesdales, they sort of looked like dragons, but didn't appear to have any scales. Looked more like lion hide, while their gargantuan wings didn't seem to have any fur at all. They did have talons, though, big eerie sharp ones, spiking out from each of their wings' large joints. And their heads, God, their heads looked like ravenous wolves. With smaller ears and a lot more teeth.

The creatures twisted and dive-bombed the craft. "Shit! Cutting right!" Garret barked. "Hold on."

But despite his swift dodging efforts, the large vessel just couldn't maneuver like its agile aggressors. Another brutal collision as one rammed them from the side, followed by multiple jarring impacts. Goddamn it. Those fuckers just latched onto the craft's wings. The screeching sound of tearing metal resounded all around.

"Motherfucker!" Kegan yelled, scrambling with the controls. "They're ripping our fucking ship apart!"

Alarmed voices instantly inundated their headpieces.

Garret hit the intercom icon. "Hold on, people. We got some unidentifieds going hostile on our asses."

"Are you shitting me?" one yelled.

"Blast the fuckers!"

"Can't!" Garret shouted. "They're not in firing range. Gonna try and throw 'em with a spin maneuver instead."

Kegan shot him a wary look. "Sure that's wise with the right engine out?"

"Got a better idea?"

Kegan cursed and shook his head. "Fuck. Alright. Do it."

Garret threw their vessel into a roll as they tore toward the ground, adjusting the maneuver to accommodate for the damaged burner. The monstrosities flew off with angry squawks, but the second he straightened shit out again, they were right back like white on freaking rice.

"Son of a bitch," he snarled. "That didn't deter them at all."

Their ship lurched violently left and right as if the creatures were playing tug of war. More ripping metal, followed by electrical blasts. Blood-curdling screeches penetrated the cabin.

Kegan grinned through tense features. "Sounds like they just shocked the shit out of themselves."

More blaring alarms wailed to life, red lights flashing over the entire navigation panel.

"That's not all they did," Garret bit out, eyeing the left engine's display. "Those ornery bastards just took out our last burner." His hands flew with purpose from one control to the next, then once again hit the intercom. "Prepare for impact, boys. Gonna be making an emergency landing."

"Five hundred feet," Kegan shouted. "And I don't see anywhere even remotely open!"

"Me, neither. Goddamn it. All fucking forest."

"Nose dipping hard! We're coming in fast!"

"Gonna cut the craft vertical, Kegan, to slice between as many of these trees on the way down as possible. Help me hold her steady."

Kegan nodded anxiously, grimacing as they tore toward a never-ending sea of treetops. "Alright. Let's do this. Two hundred feet and dropping fast."

"Twisting her ninety degrees NOW!"

Angry screeches resounded as they knifed into the foliage. Jesus, the beasts' claws were like nails scraping down a chalkboard as they begrudgingly released their hold. Back into the sky they flew as Garret's team plummeted in the opposite direction. Evidently, those fuckers were too damn big to fly through such densely wooded areas. In rapid succession, branches cracked and snapped, spider-webbing the craft's reinforced windshield.

"Initiating emergency shock absorbers! Everyone better have their fucking helmets on!"

"Fifty feet! Forty!" Kegan yelled. "Twenty-five! Oh, shit! Brace! Brace! Brace!"

Garret squinted hard as the ground flew up to meet them, impact coming fast and hard.

"Uh!" Air punched from his lungs.

Then silence.

Groaning, he gingerly turned to his co-pilot. "Fuck me... Kegan... You okay?"

Kegan nodded stiffly and grimaced. "Yeah, man. I'm okay. Gonna be feeling that for a while, though."

Through their earpieces, other unhappy voices emerged.

"Motherfucking son of a bitch..."

"Jesus. I don't *ever* wanna do *that* again."

"Shit. My helmet's busted. I think it's fucking leaking."

Garret reached forward and quickly ran tests on the environment. "S'okay. Air quality's coming up as breathable."

"Oh, thank fuck." The sound of a helmet sliding off. "Hate this big thing anyway."

More groans as unlatching harnesses resounded. Garret and Kegan unbuckled, too, and headed back into the main cabin. Four men's faces stared warily back at them.

Black-haired and blue-eyed, Paris was their tracker.

Eli was their brown-haired, brown-eyed bodyguard. As was Helix, who stood beside him, looking more than a little bit pissed. Both men were tall, cut, and covered in ink, with broad jaws and dark spiky crew cuts. Most importantly, though, and the reason they were there; both men were badass soldiers to their core.

In contrast, the team's medic was a blue-eyed blond. Sasha, the nicest, most chilled guy Garret knew. But if push came to shove, you better believe he could turn on the badass, too.

Like everyone in their unit, Garret was trained in a little bit of everything, but his primary job was that of top-dog captain. He'd quickly been recognized for his leadership skills after entering the space program with five years of first officer under his belt, but it wasn't until after he'd headed a dozen successful missions that he rose to permanent captain status. And a better-equipped captain he couldn't be with Kegan riding second in command.

Unlike Garret and his dirty-blond mane, Kegan had a head of ginger with an ever scruffy five o'clock shadow to match. And where Garret's eyes were a mix between blue and gray, Kegan's were a mix of green and gold. Sharp and efficient, he'd been Garret's right-hand man ever since Garret made it to superior. And the guy was awesome. Damn near like a brother. So yeah, Garret couldn't want for more.

Kegan eyed their flight crew. "Anybody injured?"

All shook their heads as if suddenly at a loss for words.

Paris was the first to speak up. "So what exactly was it that attacked us? Times like this make me wish we had windows back here."

Garret and Kegan swapped looks. "I dunno," Garret finally answered. "For lack of a better description, let's just say they were pterodactyls."

The team's eyebrows lifted in perfect unison.

Garret grunted. "Would you rather go with dragons?"

"As a matter of fact," Sasha chuckled apprehensively. "I actually kind of would."

"Why?" Eli muttered. "You like French-fried nuts?" He frowned at Garret. "Those fuckers weren't spouting fire, were they?"

"No, but they had some serious jaw strength. Pretty sure they tore our aircraft a new one."

Collective curses filled the cabin.

"So we're stranded here?" Helix bit out. "No better off than the dudes we came to rescue?"

"Let me check out the damage," Kegan offered. "Maybe by some miracle I'll be able to fix it."

Skeptical frowns darkened every face.

Garret exhaled as he headed over and opened the side hatch. "Paris. How far away is the distress beacon from here? Hopefully we're not too far off course."

Paris scrolled through the data bank on his bulky wristband, then tapped its screen a few more times. "Yeah. You did good, considering. It's only about four klicks north of our position."

"Four kilometers." Eli nodded, exiting the ramp. "Not too bad at all."

But as the men filed out, profanities abounded as each got a good look at the damage.

"Goddamn it," Garret growled. "They fucking shredded her."

"Maybe we should go shred them in return."

Garret looked at Helix. "I think we've got more pressing matters to deal with."

Kegan sighed, frowning at their aircraft. "Guess I'd better fire up our own distress beacon."

Garret dragged a hand down his face. He couldn't believe this shit. Was this what had happened to the first team? It'd make sense. Pilots had to be insanely skilled to qualify for missions like these, so no way had it been from inept flying. Too bad distress signals couldn't send out specifics. Because if those creatures are what took down the first crew too, then what's to stop the same thing from happening to all other rescue teams that came? Nothing. There was no real way to give headquarters a heads up. The distance for communications was just too far.

Fuck it. If home base had any brains at all, they'd be able to read between the lines. Two units down right off the bat? Hello, something was definitely going on. If the second-round rescue team didn't come with guns blazing, Garret was seriously going to kick some idiot ass.

Gripping his hips, he turned to the team. "Alright, guys. Clearly there'll be no fixing Charlotte today. So gear up with as much as you can possibly carry, and let's get moving while there's still ample light."

CHAPTER TWO

* * *

ONE YEAR EARLIER
Astrum Industries Science & Exploration
Location: Planet Nira rainforest, after emergency landing

"Emergency landing, my ass," Chet bit out irritably. "Is that seriously how you're gonna log it?"

Co-pilot, Zaden Ryes, cut their bodyguard a sharp look. "Yeah. I am. Got a problem with that?"

"Actually I do, since we straight-up fucking *crashed*." The accusation in his tone was impossible to miss. He blamed the pilots for the state they were in.

Alec Hamlin, first officer in command, turned from inspecting the wreckage. "You want full disclosure, Chet? Fine. Be my guest. Go on, tell headquarters we were attacked by *dragons*. I'm sure once you do your credibility will soar—right after they tie your ass up in a straitjacket and toss you in a padded fucking cell."

Chet scowled, but didn't say anything more, just broodingly got back to gathering his gear. Massive, ripped, with a mean looking skull cut— and gray eyes as sharp as razors—he wasn't one people made a habit of messing with. Or getting on the bad side of. But Alec didn't give a shit. He had bigger things to worry about than if soldier boy was PMSing. For fuck's sake, Chet wasn't the only one marooned on this fucking planet.

Dragging a hand through his light brown hair, Alec exchanged unsettled looks with his second in command. Zaden just shook his head and turned back to logging the report. Got to get all the details down while shit was still fresh in the head. Not that they'd be read for another year.

Alec cursed under his breath and walked over to the team's three scientists. "You guys packed up and ready to move? Once we find a place to set up camp, we can go out and do a little exploring." He sighed and scanned their alien surroundings. "God knows we have plenty of time."

"Technically," Noah pointed out, tightening his small ponytail. "One year is *not* plenty of time. At least not to those in the scientific community." The American beauty, with his honey blond hair and brown eyes, was as attractive as he was intelligent. Or in other words, a hot fucking nerd. At least, that's what the girls—and guys alike—always said.

"Yeah," Bailey chuckled, chocolate curls framing his face. "If anything, we'd call it not *enough* time."

Alec stared at him incredulously. By that happy gleam in his hazel eyes, he'd say Bailey didn't mind that they were stranded. Or that it'd take twelve months on this potentially dangerous planet before any kind of rescue team came to get them.

Shaking his head, Alec turned to Jamis. "What about you? You the only scientist here who's still got some sense?"

Jamis looked up with a smirk, brushing dark bangs from his eyes. "Sorry, Cap. Guess our rough little landing gave me brain damage, too."

Alec chuckled humorlessly and rubbed his brow. "You guys are nuts, but at least someone's happy. Just be ready to head out in five."

* * *

Right on time, less than ten minutes later, every man had every rucksack packed to go. Tromping along like the others in cargo shorts and a tank top, Alec kept steady pace with his co-pilot.

"I activated the distress beacon," Zaden informed him, studying the vicinity.

With a rich tan, black hair, and equally dark eyes, the man looked right at home. And in a way he kind of was. Having spent his childhood in Central America, he regularly traversed regions much like this. In truth, this place was just like the Amazon jungle, except not only were the dense trees taller and thicker, but were solely in all dark shades.

Green and purple mostly, with blossoms of orange and red. The flora looked a lot glossier, too, as if everything was covered in honey. Which would explain that wild honey scent Alec detected. A smell he'd picked up the second he stepped off their aircraft. Luckily for his team, the air was breathable. Luckier still was that the temperatures were accommodating. Hell, it was downright sultry as shit. Because, hello, they were in a fucking jungle.

"Good," Alec replied, stepping over a downed tree. "Hopefully it won't take long for its signal to get picked up."

"Shouldn't," Zaden muttered, peering over his shoulder. "Got the thing running at full strength." He looked back at Alec with a strange expression. "You feel that?"

Alec frowned. "Feel what? I don't feel anything."

"Like we're being watched."

Alec tensed and shot Zaden a disquieted look. The man was famous for his wicked sixth sense. "Seriously?"

Z gave a small nod, eyes combing more intently.

Alec glanced around, too. "Fucking great. Not a half hour in and we've already got company. Getting a vibe on if it's friendly or not?"

"Can't tell."

Abruptly, countless branches began snapping overhead.

"Everyone down!" Chet bit out from the front of the line. Dropping into a crouch, he aimed his rifle up at the trees.

"Don't fucking shoot!" Noah hissed. "For fuck's sake!"

Beside him, Bailey and Jamis fumbled for their mini tablets. No doubt, to get some pictures.

"Shut it," Chet growled, scanning the leafy canopy. "I'm not a goddamn idiot."

More snapping branches, getting closer, and louder. Alec and Zaden pulled out their tranq guns, too.

"It's probably just monkeys," Bailey offered. "Or big squirrels."

Everyone paused to stare at him drolly.

He scowled. "Fuck every one of you. You know what I mean."

A loud thump sounded from somewhere nearby, as if a creature of substantial weight just dropped to the ground from a tree branch high above.

"Shit," Chet barked out. "I can't tell if it's just one or a whole fucking ton of them. It's really fricking big, though. That much I know. Bossman and Z, you two ready to engage?"

"Yeah," Alec called. "Locked and loaded."

"But don't fire," Noah repeated. "Unless absolutely necessary! If they're even half as intelligent as us, we gotta try peaceful interaction first."

"Intelligence," Zaden murmured, eyeing the woods, "isn't necessarily a good thing. More often than not, it's the opposite."

"Beesha," came a deep voice from somewhere close behind.

The team leapt up and spun around as a tall figure emerged from the foliage.

Alec froze. Not only was the male before them frickin' huge—easily seven feet tall—but every single inch of his muscular body was the deepest, darkest shade of purple. Just like the trees and large bushes he stood by. Well, except for his hair, which was entirely black, made up of long, velvety dreadlocks. Not the typical, matted dreadlocks, though. In fact, Alec wasn't even sure it was hair at all. More like something that'd hurt like a bitch if someone ever tried to cut it.

He eyed the male's attire next, aka his one article of clothing. Kind of looked like a black rawhide kilt, but not as long, and with a thick matching belt. It also only hung down in the front and back, leaving the sides of his dark thighs bare. Besides black sandals and shin guards, that was all that he sported, but his upper body definitely hadn't been neglected. Biceps and wrist cuffs of the same black material, a kind of leather choker, and some piercings. Through his nipples and nasal septum, up the ridge of his ears, as well as along his... were those *horns?* Alec eyed the small, black protrusions where they emerged from his temples and curved toward the back of his head. Yup, definitely horns, but evidently pliant enough to withstand being pierced repeatedly.

The male met Alec's eyes, as if feeling his stare, and his dark, full lips slowly curved. Fangs. The dude had huge fucking fangs. Jesus, he was intimidating. Even to a guy like Alec who'd fought in countless wars, and who wasn't exactly small himself. But humans, whether ally or adversary, just couldn't compare to this brute. He was thick. And dense. Just all around *big*. Even his facial features were large. Strong nose. Square jaw. High, pronounced cheekbones. Not to mention that broad, firm mouth. Or those huge, piercing eyes that were boring into Alec's with irises of churning gold.

"Beesha," he repeated, turning his gaze to the others. When all they did was stand there and gape—while Chet held him brazenly in his crosshairs—the male lifted his hand, fingers tipped with small, black claws, and made a nonviolent gesture. "Kerra... Móonday... Reesha tay..."

The team swapped looks, then all eyes turned to Alec. Right. Because with no one able to translate, this shit defaulted to the captain. Not sensing any immediate danger—probably because Chet's rifle was still trained on the big dude's head—Alec tucked his tranq gun back into his leg holster, cleared his throat, and lifted his hands, too. "Um... Hello... We... uh... come in peace."

A collective groan rose up from his team.

"Seriously?" Jamis groused.

Noah grimaced. "Beyond lame."

"Oh, yeah?" Alec scowled. "Well, then why don't *you* do it, Mr. Peaceful Interaction?"

Noah stiffened, but before he could say a word, the male's amused chuff stole their attention.

"Moyos ochay," he rumbled, grinning wide. "Ochay kuntah kai."

The team watched him blankly, then one by one started to smile.

"He's friendly." Bailey exhaled in clear relief. "Scary as shit, but friendly."

The male stepped forward. Everyone tensed. So he paused again and inclined his head. "Gesh," he stated, pointing to himself. Then he extended a hand in their direction and eyed each team member expectantly.

"His name is Gesh." Jamis' smile spread wider. "He wants to know our names, too."

"Thanks for that, Einstein," Chet muttered in agitation. "Why don't you do the introductions."

Jamis swallowed and looked back over at Alec. "I would, but we should probably let the captain do it, so it's clear who's in charge of our unit."

Great. Cursing under his breath, Alec resumed addressing the giant. "Uh... I am Alec," he started, pointing to himself. Then he motioned to the rest of his crew. "And this here is Zaden, and Chet, and Bailey. And those two are Noah and Jamis."

Gesh listened intently, regarding each one, his gaze lingering longest on Noah. Again, he inclined his head and smiled. "Enday myah. Bukah chay." His eyes slid to Chet and his gun. "Móotah may," he murmured darkly.

Noah shifted, as if still feeling the effects of Gesh's stare. "He doesn't like Chet pointing that gun at his face."

"I wouldn't, either," Bailey muttered.

"Yeah, well, too fucking bad," Chet grunted. "Are you not seeing the size of this fucking behemoth? Or that he's got fricking fangs and claws?"

Gesh pursed his lips, as if understanding Chet's words.

For the first time since their new friend's arrival, Zaden spoke up, his gaze locked on Gesh. "He's smart. Really smart. Might even know what we're saying."

"But is he safe?" Alec asked. "Are we cool? Can we trust him?"

"I dunno." Zaden frowned. "I still can't tell."

Noah raked a hand through his flyaway bangs. "Come on, guys. There's six of us and only one of him. And he's not the one with the guns. I say we ease up a little. Let the guy breathe."

Chet looked at Alec. "Your call, Boss."

Alec exhaled and scrubbed his face. "Stand down, Chet, but keep your eye on our friend—and your gun's safety permanently off."

"Roger that," Chet muttered, lowering his weapon.

Immediately, Gesh's big broad smile returned, his huge fangs back in full view. "Bellah," he rumbled brightly, then gestured for them to follow as he turned and started walking.

As one, the three scientists looked at Alec. "We're gonna go with him, right?" Bailey asked almost urgently.

"Yeah," Jamis chimed in. "Since he's a big reason we came."

"Who knows," Noah added, sweetening the pot. "Maybe he'll find us a cool place to camp."

Alec chuckled and gave a nod. "Okay. Fine. Whatever. Chet, stay at Gesh's back."

Chet glared the giant's way as they all started walking. "Nowhere I'd rather be."

* * *

For the next couple of hours, they hiked the lush terrain, stopping every so often for a breather. Good thing they all were in stellar shape or those stops would've been way more frequent.

Alec kept a close eye on Gesh as he interacted with the science trio. They told him about Earth, how they were humans, about their wreck. Gesh told them about his planet, Nira, too. From his gestures, they were able to discern it wasn't all jungle. And that his specific species was Kríe.

He also showed them plants and pointed to critters, offering up lots of strange names. And the threesome ate up every bit of it. The way their faces lit with wonder as they captured images and gathered countless samples…

Alec smiled. The sight of them brimming with so much tangible joy almost made the whole crash worthwhile. Almost. Because, like Jamis said, Gesh was a large reason for why they'd come. Gesh and this great big uncharted world. So even though their aircraft sat in utter shambles, their bottom-line mission felt successful.

Gesh brought them to another stop, this time at the opening of a clearing. It was small, but with that running brook a few yards away, it'd make a perfect place to camp. Just enough space to pitch their personal tents and settle in good before nightfall.

Gesh squatted down at the creek and scooped some water with his hands. Looking over his shoulder, he grinned at the team. "Reesa," he stated, taking a hardy drink.

Alec eyed his empty water bottle, then gestured to Jamis. "Check it."

Jamis nodded, pulled off his rucksack, and quickly rummaged inside. A couple seconds later, he found what he wanted and headed over to kneel down at the stream. Scooping up a sample of the liquid, he tested it in a small container. "Looks good. No protozoa. No bacteria. No viruses."

Gesh paused and gave an indignant grunt. "Tah." He nodded, scooping up some more. "Reesa bellah kai."

Alec watched the Kríe drink for another few minutes before finally giving his guys the green light. "Alright. Fill your canteens, and a couple extras, too."

Bailey was first to partake of the water. Noah wasn't far behind. Sinking to his haunches right beside Gesh, the blond scientist smiled at the Kríe. Gesh paused and returned the friendly gesture, his gold gaze once again lingering. As if there was something about Noah in particular that intrigued him.

Chet replenished quickly while Gesh continued drinking, then got back to watch-dogging their guide. Alec smirked and shook his head as he made his way to the brook. Their hired gun was nothing if not efficient.

Gesh finished a second later, stood, and looked around till his eyes locked on a stand of purple trees. Dark gaze glittering, he approached them, lips curved. The scientists swapped looks, then followed him over.

"Tah..." Gesh rumbled, reaching for a deep maroon blossom—which there were tons of, running up each glossy trunk. Clutching one of its huge, plump petals, he squeezed it with his clawed thumb and forefinger. Thick juice instantly oozed from the spot, releasing more of that super-sweet scent. Gesh licked his fingers and looked at the trio. "Tukah?" he asked, rubbing his lean abs.

All three guys eyed the flower hesitantly.

"Um... Are we?" Bailey turned and looked at his colleagues. "Hungry for syrupy flowers?"

But before his friends could give a reply, Gesh barked out a deep, rich laugh. "Mah." He shook his head. "Mah, moyos ochay." Grinning, he pointed up to a cluster of eggplant-looking fruit.

"Oh." Bailey chuckled.

Noah and Jamis cracked up laughing.

Observing from the creek, Alec watched Gesh scale the tree. A couple ticks after he disappeared into the canopy, countless globes started to drop.

Zaden stopped beside Alec and crossed his arms. "Drink and now food. He's being very hospitable."

Alec motioned for Jamis to check the fruit, then turned to look at his friend. "He makes you uneasy."

Zaden nodded. "Yeah. He does." He scanned the trees above as well as the surrounding brush. "Why is he out here all alone? And why was he so eager to befriend us?"

Alec crossed his arms, too, and gave a shrug. "Maybe he's just curious about us, like we are of him. Maybe his species travel alone. Like male lions. Roaming solo instead of with a pride."

"If that was the case, then again I ask, why is he so intent on being with us? Why not just watch us from a distance?"

Alec scratched his cheek, lacking an answer. "I dunno. I mean, while lion males are typically loners, they do hang out in groups from time to time."

Zaden turned and pinned him with suspicious eyes. "Only when they want to mate."

Alec coughed out a laugh. "Okay, maybe male lions were a bad analogy."

"Fruit's safe," Jamis announced, holding up another vial. "No toxins, poisons, bacteria, bugs…"

Gesh dropped down, then settled against the tree and grinned at his ample pile. "Mah, mahn besh," he rumbled low. "Senna`sohnsay bellah kai."

One by one, he tossed them all fruit. The team looked at Alec. Alec looked at Gesh. All but rolling his eyes, the Kríe took a huge bite and started chewing away. Zaden shifted his weight restlessly. To their left, Chet's stomach growled.

"I *am* fucking starving," their hired guard muttered. He looked at Alec. "And the stuff's cool, right?"

Alec swapped looks with Zaden, then glanced back at Gesh. Gesh smiled and took another big bite. "Bellah," he repeated. "Bellah kai."

Noah watched their guide eat. "Bellah kai," he mused. "Got the feeling that means very good."

Gesh grinned and nodded at the golden blond. "Tah, Noah. 'Gewd.' Moyo eenta."

Noah beamed. "I think he just called me smart."

"Awesome," Chet drawled. "Looks like you've got yourself a translator, Boss. Now, can I eat this purple thingy or what?"

Right on cue, Gesh chomped another mouthful, his strong jaw chewing away.

"Okay," Alec relented. "But don't eat too much. We've got plenty of rations in our sacks."

"Gonna be here for a while, Cap," Jamis reminded. "Might wanna save those for later."

Chet sat on a downed log and took a tentative bite. "Ohhh… Oh, my God. Tastes like peaches."

"Damn," Bailey moaned, trying it, too. "Like the perfectly ripe, super-sweet white ones."

Noah settled into a spot between Bailey and Gesh, his own fruit clutched in hand. "No shit?"

"Oh, yeah. No shit. For reals."

"*Yes.* I fucking *love* the white ones."

Alec shook his head and smiled, sitting down beside Chet. Zaden joined him while the trio remained with Gesh. Zaden still looked uneasy, but before too long, everyone was happily chowing down. Alec sighed, tension easing. Maybe with their big, strong guide around, surviving for a year wouldn't be too hard. God, he couldn't wait to pitch his tent, make a fire, and just relax.

Allowing his mind to wander, he gazed up at a tiny opening high in the canopy above, where two small, winged creatures flittered about. Kind of funny how they reminded him of over-sized betta fish. He watched them playing and didn't look back down again until Gesh's dark chuckle seized his attention. Alec eyed the male, then glanced at his team. Like him, each had finished nearly all of his fruit while Gesh sat smugly looking on. No, scratch that. He didn't look just smug. That grin of his was downright leering.

Zaden stiffened at Alec's side.

Chet cursed and raised his rifle. "Why the fuck is he looking at us like that?"

A louder, hardier laugh rose from Gesh's chest. "Moyos mahneenta. Mahneenta kai."

Face paling, Noah slowly turned to Alec. "I think he just called us stupid."

Alec's heart skipped a beat, then took off racing. But before he could even mutter, *oh shit*, a burning pinch lanced through his shoulder. Alec hissed as his teammates jerked in similar pain, alarmed shouts filling his ears. Alec looked down at his shoulder. What the friggin' fuck? A tiny dart was lodged into his muscle. And the fucker stung like hell. Scowling he tugged it free, but the damage was already done, his vision darkening rapidly.

Beside him, Zaden groaned, then flopped to the ground. Chet was quick to follow. Heart fumbling in panic, Alec looked back to Gesh where the huge Kríe sat grinning bigger than shit.

Oh, God. Oh, no. They were so fucking screwed. Then everything went black.

CHAPTER THREE

* * *

Alec roused to the crackle and popping of a fire… and the sound of more than one Gesh-like voice. Eyelids not quite ready to open, he shifted with a groan. Then froze. Somehow he was sitting upright but couldn't move. Not much at least, thanks to something holding him secure by his throat and chest. Heart instantly back to hammering, he forced his eyes to open so he could get busy assessing what the fuck. Slowly, his blurry vision started to clear. It was nighttime and, oh God, he was tied to a tree.

Trying not to freak, he looked down at his body. Well, attempted to at least, which wasn't easy with rope holding his neck against a trunk. Meaning, he couldn't see the other rope, either. The one wound tightly across his chest, and underneath both of his armpits. Normally, a wrap like that would allow arm movement, but unfortunately that wasn't the case. Because with knees bent and open, Alec's wrists and ankles were tied and bound together with only a scant bit of rope between them. Which allowed Alec to lift his hands a little, but not straighten out his legs.

Fucking great.

That'd definitely make escaping a challenge.

Instinctively, he tugged at his snugly tied hands. But when his wrists and forearms grazed his crotch, he made another startling discovery. His dick was literally hard as rock, and his nut sac felt kind of swollen, too. What the fuck? Had he been having a wet dream while knocked out cold? Talk about messed up timing.

Warily, he lifted his eyes to his surroundings. A half-dozen yards away, poking at a campfire, Gesh sat talking to… *another* Kríe. Alec sucked in a breath as his eyes focused more. Oh, hell. Make that *three* other Kríe. And all of them were ransacking the team's rucksacks! Alec glowered.

Then five more Kríe strode into view.

Aw, fuck. Tied up and totally outnumbered.

Heart pounding faster, Alec looked for his men. Didn't take him long to find them bound to trees, too. The science trio was still completely out. Most likely because their slightly smaller builds had yet to work off the sedatives. But Zaden and Chet were wide fucking awake, glaring poison daggers at their captors.

Zaden glanced his way and met Alec's gaze, his dark eyes all kinds of stressed. As they should be. Their team was in big fucking trouble. And Alec had no clue what to do. Gesh and his buddies had stripped them of their possessions, so there was no chance a pocket knife would still be in his shorts. Not that he could reach it if it was. Truth be told, he didn't really want to move his hands anyway. His cock was too sensitive to handle more contact; needed some alone time to chill.

Zaden gestured to his own bound wrists and wiggled his index finger. Alec blinked at the thing, confused at first, until Z started to tap it in a pattern. Ah. Of course. Morse Code. Alec should've thought of that himself. In his defense, though, he was still kind of groggy around the edges. Intently, he tried to focus on that finger, frowning when Zaden stopped and made a strange face. But when Z shifted his hips awkwardly, Alec instantly understood. He looked back at Zaden's hands, or more specifically, the straining fly he was trying so hard not to touch.

What the hell?

Alec glanced at the others, discovering they, too, were sporting huge frickin' bulges. Even the threesome still snoozing away. Zaden cleared his throat, ready to resume, but Alec was still wrapping his brain around what was going on. Forcing his focus back on Z, Alec studied his friend's tapping finger. But before he could make out a single sentiment, none other than Gesh sauntered over.

Grinning, the big fucker squatted down in front of him, his skin looking black in the firelight. "Alec," he greeted, his rich timbre smug.

"Asshole," Alec irritably returned.

Gesh canted his head, his expression amused, then reached out and ran a claw down Alec's forearm. Not hard enough to draw blood, but enough to warrant Alec's attention. Because that black little fucker was sharp. Alec watched it warily until Gesh used it to lift Alec's chin, forcing Alec's gaze back to his. Alec studied his face, his features inexplicably attractive, that tiny hoop through his nasal septum only adding to his exotic appeal. And God, up close, his golden eyes were amazing—even if Alec *was* pissed at the guy. Stunning. Damn near hypnotizing. Especially with his black pupils all dilated like that.

Again, Gesh's lips curved into a grin. "I was impatient for you to wake, Alec. Was impatient for us to talk."

Alec blinked, then froze. Holy shit. Gesh spoke English. But wait. No way that was possible.

Gesh chuffed out a laugh, his grin expanding until thick fangs dropped into view. Wow, for such a bastard, the Kríe had a great smile. The way those full, dark lips made the white of his teeth pop...

Alec squeezed his eyes shut and tried to clear his head. God, not only was he hearing things, but wearing rose-colored glasses, too. Gesh did *not* have a great smile. Gesh was a backstabbing dick.

Gesh's next laugh came out noticeably deeper. "I never stabbed your back. And while my "dick" is substantial, I do not believe that makes me one as a whole."

Alec's mouth dropped open, the last of his haze evaporating. "Oh, my God. You're translating telepathically." He searched the Kríe's face, unable to believe it. "But how are you cracking our language barrier?"

Gesh shrugged a beefy shoulder. "It is something we all do."

Alec eyed him incredulously.

Gesh tilted his head. "For a species with such advanced technology, your brains are not very developed."

Alec narrowed his eyes. "Uh huh. Nice dodge. Do you even know how you do it?"

Gesh relented with a chuckle. "Yes. Of course. Our minds break down discourse, process words into basic sentiments. In turn, we project our own thoughts back on a brain wave that is compatible to all species."

Alec frowned. "So how come we couldn't understand you before?"

"I suspect because you had not yet eaten Niran food."

Alec stared at him blankly, not quite following.

Gesh grinned and shook his head. "When it entered your bloodstream, it woke a part of your brain that your kind has not yet started using. The part that enables higher communication."

Whoa. The trio was going to have a field day with that. But unfortunately, Alec couldn't. Not while they were in such dire straits.

He glanced at Zaden, who was watching them intently, then turned his attention back to Gesh. "Fine. Whatever. Nice fucking trick. Why were you waiting on *me?*"

"You are leader of your unit, are you not?"

Alec pursed his lips. "Why are you doing this? Why trick us and hold us captive?"

Another idle shrug. "Because I can."

Gesh looked down to watch his claw resume its roaming. Along Alec's inner elbow, back down his forearm, then across the meaty base of his thumb. But it wasn't until that claw grazed Alec's straining bulge that his body gave a head-to-toe shiver.

Gesh looked up and smiled. "You are sensitive here." Slowly, he ran his finger up Alec's fly.

Alec moaned. Then glared. "Yeah. I am. So stop touching and give me a better answer."

Gesh smirked and inched closer. "I tricked you because I want your team. But you were skittish. And had many weapons."

Had being the operative word. They didn't have shit now but the clothes on their backs.

Alec scowled. "But *why* do you want us? Maybe we can make a deal."

Again, Gesh chuffed. "Moyo ochay." *Funny creature.* An utterance Alec remembered from earlier. Gesh lifted his paw and ran a knuckle along Alec's jaw, then slid his fingers into Alec's hair. "I want your team because I find you delicious. Your species is very alluring."

Idly, he grazed his claws along Alec's scalp. Goosebumps instantly flared to life. Alec shivered again. Damn. He was super-sensitized everywhere. He tried to dislodge Gesh's fingers from his hair but couldn't move his head enough to do so.

Frustrated and restless, he glowered at his captor. "So what does that mean? You want us as some kind of yummy little prey to play cat and mouse with in your jungle?"

Gesh lifted a dark brow. "Intriguing, but no. That is not what I have in mind."

"Then what," Alec grated. "Gonna kill us and stuff us? So you can stick us up all pretty on your mantle?"

Gesh's fangs flashed in the firelight as he leaned in closer, his woodsy scent enveloping Alec's senses. "What I want is much more indulgent than that." He dragged his hot tongue up Alec's cheek.

Alec froze. "Oh, God. You're gonna eat us."

Gesh stilled, then leaned back and let loose a laugh. A big, deep, jaunty one, and genuine as hell. "You are comical, human. But not very bright."

Alec bristled. "I don't know your fucking culture. You could all be a bunch of cannibals." He paused and eyed Gesh warily. "You're not a bunch of cannibals, right?"

"No." Gesh resumed his lazy lapping, this time up Alec's jaw to his ear.

"Ah!" Alec grimaced. "Stop fucking licking me. Goddamn. And just tell me what you want."

Gesh growled against his skin. "As if I owe you an explanation. You are nothing more than playthings, Alec. Playthings to delight in as we wish." He cupped Alec's crotch and bit down on his lobe.

Alec gasped, his junk going bat-shit crazy as every drop of blood drained from his face. "Holy shit," he rasped. "You… Your team… You're going to force yourselves on us sexually."

Gesh jerked back as if offended, then slowly grinned. "Oh, no, delicious creature. You will gladly consent. In fact, you will *beg* us for our cocks."

Alec grit his teeth. "Never gonna happen."

Gesh lifted a brow, canted his head, and eyed Alec's obvious bulge. "You do not think?"

"No," Alec snapped. "I do not fucking think."

Gesh's lips twitched. "We shall see." His thumb brushed Alec's crotch—right atop his sensitive glans.

Alec inhaled sharply, then paused in realization, nailing Gesh with another irate glare. "*You* did this to us, you twisted fuck."

Gesh's big eyes gleamed.

Alec seethed harder. "How."

"Senna`sohnsay," Gesh purred. *Fruit of unrelenting fire.*

Alec blinked. "You mean, that fruit you fed us? But… I watched you eat it, too."

Again, Gesh shrugged. "It is not poison."

"Yeah, but you're obviously immune."

"Am I?"

Gesh curled his big paw around Alec's bound hands and pressed them against his own crotch. Then, as if to hammer things home, he slowly moved them up his length. Alec gaped. He couldn't help it. Was too fucking floored. Because not only did Gesh's cock feel harder than steel, but longer than a fucking pole. The distance from its base to its bulging crown seemed to go on forever. Easily twelve inches, probably more, with the girth of a baseball bat on steroids.

Alec shook his head as much as he could move it. "I don't understand. Why would you subject yourself, too?"

"Because it was the only way to convince your team to eat. And besides, I like the feeling."

Wholly disturbed, Alec shifted his hips, his own cock growing more sensitive. "Great. And how long does "the feeling" last?"

"It will not relent until seed has spilled."

Alec exhaled in relief. Oh, thank fuck. He could easily rub one off. As could his team.

Gesh's eyes bore into his. "So you see, you are not alone. I too ache for release." He dragged his tongue slowly down his fang. "Would you like to help me with this?"

Alec stilled, then grimaced. "Ah, God, dude. No. Go jerk off behind a damn tree."

Gesh canted his head, brows furrowing at Alec's words, a hint of confusion flickering in his gaze. "But that will not do any good."

Alec chuckled darkly. "Hey, not my problem. You got yourself into this mess. Untie me and maybe I'll help you find a woman."

"A *woman?*" Gesh repeated, eyeing Alec oddly. Standing up, he squeezed his junk. "You speak no sense, but I do not care. It is too soon for you to truly understand. Tonight I will sate my body's needs elsewhere." Pivoting on his heel, he called to one of his pack. "Roni. Reckay óondah. Nenya rhya may tai." *Roni. I need release. Come fuck me now.*

Gee, how nice of him to translate that, too. But wait a minute. Gesh wanted *Roni* to fuck him? He wasn't going to find a female? Alec supposed he shouldn't be surprised with the way Gesh had acted. The massive Kríe must swing both ways. Which made sense in a way, since he only traveled with males. But hold up. Shouldn't *Gesh* be fucking *Roni*, and not the other way around? Gesh was the one who needed to come.

Confused, Alec watched a male pause from ransacking Chet's pack to follow Gesh into the woods. Not far, however, just barely out of sight. Not out of Alec's sight, though. Guess Gesh wanted to give him a good show.

Alec wanted to turn away but was too morbidly curious. The fact that he was horny as hell probably didn't help. Swallowing, he watched the two Kríe get busy. Roni shoved Gesh face-first against a tree, then grabbed Gesh's kilt and yanked it off. He wasn't exactly gentle, either. Seemed to enjoy getting nice and rough. Gesh seemed to enjoy that shit a lot too, going by the grin on his face. Alec could literally see his thick fangs flashing a dozen yards away. But those teeth only distracted Alec for a second. All too soon, he was completely enraptured by the sight of Gesh's incredible physique. Man, he was ripped—in all the right places. Even his ass was friggin' perfect.

Roni palmed said cheeks, then smacked one wicked hard, sending a *crack!* through the darkness. Team members and Kríe paused to turn toward the sound. But only Alec was in a position to see.

Roni tore off his own little black kilt next and grabbed his massive cock. It too was rock hard, jutting up like a cannon. Fisting its base, he squeezed and pulled up, precum emerging instantly from its head. Glistening and thick, so much welled free, Alec could see the stuff no problem from where he sat. And, holy fuck, was there a lot. Guess dicks that big needed lots of extra lube.

Roni tugged Gesh's lower body away from the trunk and slid his cockhead up and down Gesh's crack. Which evidently was sufficient enough to slick things up, because two seconds later, Gesh howled through the forest as Roni rammed his dick nice and deep. But even nice and deep, the male still had a ways to go, considering the length of his shaft. Further, further, he shoved into Gesh's depths, until all twelve plus inches of him were gone.

And then his glutes got busy, flexing as he thrust in and out. Gesh clawed at the tree bark, even tried to fang it, as he took Roni's sensual beating.

Alec shuddered, the visual intense. Insane. Utterly fucking erotic. Pressure rose steadily up his cock—till Alec froze in realization of what he was doing. Rubbing one off while he watched two dudes fuck? What the fuck was wrong with him? A new low, even for him. But in his defense, that fruit Gesh fed them was seriously kicking his ass. Alec glanced back over at the two Kríe banging. Ah hell, Gesh's swaying cock was oozing precum, too. He also had a pained expression on his face, but not the bad kind of pain. The kind one got when he needed to come.

Alec shifted his hips and grit out a curse. God, he needed to come, too.

Abruptly, Roni pulled free and spun Gesh around, only to shove him right back against the tree. Then he bent down and hooked his forearms behind Gesh's knees and hefted Gesh's feet off the ground. Legs secured in the crooks of his elbows, Roni shoved back inside Gesh and resumed pounding. Gesh grasped the tree behind his head, as if needing something sturdy to hold on to. Which he probably did, with the way Roni was slamming him.

Alec groaned, imagining how good Roni's dick must feel. But then the Kríe flat-out shocked him sideways. With his arms bearing all of Gesh's weight, Roni grasped his partner's cock with both hands and brought the thing to his mouth. He tongued it, teethed it, sucked it as he thrust. Gesh craned his head to the side, the campfire's light illuminating his raw, blissed-out features.

Holy fuck, this was way too intense. Alec's hips jerked as his bound hands once again squeezed his cock. Shit, his nuts ached so damn bad.

Closing his knees, he restlessly glanced around. No one was looking his way. His heart raced haphazardly as he warred with himself. Because a very big part of his brain right now was telling him to screw it and juice his monkey. Who cared if it was to the tune of two Kríe males rutting. It was either that or lose his ever-loving mind. Desperate times, desperate measures, and all that jazz. Besides, with the way his cock was reeling, he could probably get the job done in seconds.

Eyes back on the fuck fest, Alec palmed his crotch and discreetly got busy rubbing.

Oh, yeah. Ah, shit. That felt incredible. His eyes rolled back on a deep-throated moan, but snapped right back open when Roni snarled. Damn, he had Gesh's back arching hard, with his dick still lodged in Roni's mouth. The male pounded faster, then faster still. So, fuck yeah, Alec matched his pace. Up and down, up and down, he furiously rubbed, the heel of his palm getting hot.

So close, oh God, he was so fucking close.

His body started shaking, little jerks and bucks, but still he stayed teetering on the edge. Shit, maybe he *did* need to pull the thing out. Again, he glanced around, and again no one was looking. The trio, still out cold. Z and Chet, beyond busy glaring venom at the males going through their stuff. Alec yanked down his fly with trembling hands and pulled out his throbbing cock. Gripping it tight, he got back to stroking, working it between twitching thighs.

Another restless groan rolled up his throat as his lungs began to pant. Oh yeah, this was better. Fuck, so fucking good... His eyes locked back onto Gesh and Roni. For some reason he wanted to blow his load right when Gesh finally did. Which, by the look of things, was going to happen soon. Gesh was flat-out shuddering in Roni's hold. His hands left the shredded bark and sank into Roni's dreads. Roni snarled around his dick, probably because Gesh was clawing his scalp. Alec watched them raptly, pumping faster, no longer able to look away.

Oh, shit... Oh, shit... He needed to come.

And then Gesh arched so fucking hard, he was forced to cling back to the tree. Clearly, it was either that, or slide off as he came. And the big Kríe was definitely coming. Alec could see his cock pulsing, powering cum up its shaft, straight into Roni's waiting mouth. On and on, he kept unloading as, in turn, Roni kept fucking him raw. Damn. How much jizz did these fuckers make?

Alec hissed at the mind-blowing scene before him, and furiously pumped to bust his nut, too. But damn it, he couldn't get over that ridge. His teeth clenched feverishly. He refused to give up. Even when Roni eased things to slow-and-steady as he finished off the last of Gesh's load.

Yes, Alec needed to come like *that*. But no matter how fast he pumped, or how high his nuts climbed, he couldn't get his orgasm to come. So damn close, but ever out of reach. Gasping in agony, he tugged his knees close and gave up with a miserable moan. Shit, now his whole body hurt like a mother. Worst fucking idea ever.

Grimacing, he panted through vicious pangs, eyes squeezed shut, not wanting to see another second. Of what Gesh was able to find just now that Alec absolutely couldn't. Completion. Orgasmic bliss. But ultimately, relief.

A dark, sated chuckle brushed past his ears. Alec peered up, lashes damp, to find Gesh standing in front of him. His kilt was back on, but he was still breathing heavy, the firelight revealing a thin sheen of sweat.

His hooded gaze dropped to eye Alec's cock, still out and straining for release. "Perhaps you would like a little help? It appears your attempt did not work."

Unable to speak, Alec flipped him off instead, then gingerly shoved his dick back into his pants. No way in hell was he fucking a guy. Or letting a guy fuck him. Especially one with a flagpole dick. Besides, the eyeful Gesh gave him was probably what messed him up. Seriously, that shit between him and Roni? Totally fucking twisted. Only reason it'd rubbed Alec right at all was because he was so horny from that fruit. All Alec needed was another go. Another lap without all the visuals. But if for some crazy reason he still couldn't bust? His body would definitely burn that fruit off. Either way, it was just a matter of time.

Gesh chuckled again as he turned to leave, his post-romp timbre deeper than ever. "Suit yourself, human, but this I promise you. Soon you will not only *want* our cocks, but will crave them above all else."

Scowling through another grimace, Alec watched him go, just as the trio started waking. And just like his had undoubtedly done, their expressions quickly ran the gamut of emotions. Drowsy confusion. Growing alarm. Shock. Then finally panic. Alec exhaled heavily. Those poor, clueless scientists had no idea how bad it truly was.

Fuck, it was going to be a really long night.

CHAPTER FOUR

* * *

Alec woke the next morning to the sound of arguing. Specifically, that of Chet and one of Gesh's cronies.

"For the last fucking time, get your paws off my shit!"

A deep, amused rumble. "You mean *my* shit."

"No, you bitch. I mean fucking mine. Touch it again and I'll kick your purple ass."

A robust laugh followed after that. "I would much enjoy seeing you try."

"Yeah? Well, untie me and I'll get right on that."

Looked like Gesh wasn't the only one head-talking with Alec's team.

Groaning softly, Alec peeled open his eyes, noting how it was barely light. And how Chet and Roni were having a glare-off. Well, Chet was glaring. Roni was brazenly smirking. Alec would've shaken his head if he could have. Unfortunately, the fact that Chet looked so wide awake meant he hadn't slept at all last night, or something had pulled him out of his slumber early.

Alec couldn't decide which prospect was worse. Just the thought of their captors being around them unsupervised made him tense. Didn't trust those bastards as far as he could throw them. And considering how much they undoubtedly weighed, he probably couldn't even heft one off the ground. But if Chet didn't sleep that would mean the poor guy most likely wasn't feeling too hot. For reasons Alec would rather not think about. Not that he couldn't already feel his morning wood raging like a beast against his fly. Although, typically, "morning wood" implied a waking freshie, and Alec's was probably the same one from last night.

He shifted against his tree post and regarded Gesh's roguish crew. In dawn's early light, he could see them much better than before with just a campfire to go by. They definitely looked very similar to Gesh, but now he saw definite differences. Like the varying designs of their body piercings, or the unique cuts and stitching of their "kilts." Even the curve to their horns differed subtly, as did the appearance of their dreads. Some were longer, or thicker, or pulled back.

Alec glanced to where he'd last seen his team, bound to their individual trees. Yup, still there, and just like Alec, they too were now wide awake. Chet's bitching worked better than his alarm clock back on base. Not that Alec begrudged him for being so pissed. For fuck's sake, thanks to those miscreants going through their stuff, they were now tied up with their own freaking rope. The irony of it was like a kick in the balls.

Gesh appeared from the trees, adjusting his kilt as if he'd just finished taking a piss. Something that Alec needed to do badly. Morning wood or not, his bladder was full. Again, he shifted uncomfortably as Gesh stopped in front of them.

"Ah. At last. You are all awake. Good. It is nearly time to go." He motioned for Roni to fetch their bottled waters.

"Where are we going?" Bailey tentatively asked.

"To your final destination."

"That doesn't sound ominous," Noah deadpanned with a frown.

Gesh peered down at him, but didn't offer reassurance. The trio shot uneasy looks Alec's way. He gave them his best don't-worry-I'll-find-a-way-out-of-this expression, then turned his gaze back to Gesh.

"Listen. I really gotta drain my bladder. Pretty sure my team does, too. So unless you wanna smell piss all day, I suggest you let us go do our business."

Gesh's lips curved wryly. "What if I like the smell of your piss?"

Alec grit his teeth. "You wouldn't. Trust me."

Gesh chuckled and motioned to another of his pack. "Miros. Gonja. Otahtah." *Miros. Take them. One at a time.*

Standing beside the campfire, Miros grunted and ambled over.

Gesh pointed to Alec. "Start with their leader."

Miros regarded Alec for a second, then squatting down, untied the rope at Alec's neck. But instead of moving on to the rope at Alec's chest, he wound that first rope into a collar. Nice and snug around Alec's throat, with the rest of it serving as a leash. Alec bristled. Gesh grinned, clearly amused by his irritation. His chest was freed next, and then his ankles, but his wrists Miros kept tightly bound.

Standing, he gave Alec's leash a tug. "Nenya, moyo," he rumbled. *Come.*

Angry and embarrassed that his team was looking on, Alec scowled and shoved to his feet. Sharp pain instantly lanced through his gut. God, it felt like his overly-full bladder was battling it out with his junk. Junk that still needed desperately to unload.

Grimacing, he followed Miros deeper into the woods, feeling his men's gazes as he went. His chest filled with heavy regret. How was he going to get them out of this mess? Realistically, their options looked pretty grim. Maybe if he could get some time alone with Chet and Zaden, they could work out a plan to escape. They had to. And before they reached "their final destination." Because otherwise, their chances to ever escape would most likely drastically drop. Alec was afraid to even consider what would come of them after that.

Miros came to a stop by a glossy-trunked tree, the thing so dark it looked almost black. Alec yanked down his fly, shoved his hand inside and grabbed his rigid cock. Potent sensation tore through his groin. Alec groaned at the feeling, then froze and looked at his escort. The fucker was expectantly staring at Alec's hand, as if dying to get a look at his package.

Alec glowered, needing so fucking bad to piss. "Really? You're not gonna give me some privacy?"

Miros chuffed a deep chuckle and crossed his arms, leaning his shoulder against a tree. "And miss a chance to see your hard cock? You could not bribe me to look away."

Alec narrowed his eyes. "Who says it's hard?"

"No one needs to." Miros' lips curved higher. "You ate senna`sohnsay and have not spilled."

"Who says I haven't spilled? Maybe I did when no one was looking."

Miros blinked, cocked his head, expression curious, then let loose a rich, hardy laugh. "Ochay moyo." *Funny creature.* "As if you could do such alone."

Alec frowned. What the fuck was that supposed to mean? Had these guys seriously never jerked off before? He couldn't even begin to imagine such a thought. Especially with how endowed they all were.

Not willing to go any further with their stupid exchange, and almost ready to piss his pants, Alec cursed in frustration and turned around, then tugged his dick from his pants. Ugh. Son of a bitch, it was so damn hard he couldn't even point it downward. Looked like he'd be making one majorly golden arch.

With Miros at his back, he closed his eyes and concentrated really hard. Because pissing with a boner wasn't ever easy, and the one he was sporting was a doozy. Seconds ticked by, and then a minute, but still not one drop of relief. Alec winced and gave his shaft a squeeze. Oh, shit. Bad idea. Now his dick was teeming harder. Relinquishing all contact except for his thumb, he inhaled deep and tried to relax. His nut sac tingled and his urethra started to burn. But no urination would be had.

Biting back a whimper, he dropped his head. "Fuck."

A dark, velvet chuckle tickled his ear. Miros, leaning close to get a look. "Your hard little cock needs some help."

Alec jerked, then glared at the Kríe over his shoulder. "It doesn't need help and it's not fucking little."

Miros lifted a dubious brow.

Alec clenched his jaw. "Just because you're enormous doesn't mean that I'm small."

Miros shrugged indifferently. "I did not say that small was bad. Would make sucking your cock that much easier."

Alec tensed as images flooded his brain of Miros giving him head until he came. His dick reeled harder in the cool morning air. The fact that he'd even envisioned that shit was not a good sign at all. The fact that a part of him would welcome a Miros blowjob was even fucking worse.

Nuts firming, he winced and turned away. "Just shut up and let me concentrate."

Miros sighed and moved to stand beside him so they both faced the same direction. "Close your eyes, Alec, and listen to the sound."

Alec frowned, but before he could ask what Miros meant, Miros pulled out his big, mighty python. Alec stared as the Kríe began to piss. He couldn't help it. Never had he seen such a giant cock up close. And, fucking hell, it wasn't even hard. Easily eight limp inches long, with the girth of a fat frickin' cucumber. Alec could only imagine what it'd look like erect. Yeah, he'd seen Roni's and Gesh's already, but that was from a dozen yards away. Near like this, he got a better sense of its true size, and saw some other distinguishing traits, too. Like how it lacked foreskin and surrounding pubic hair. Or how its crown—in relation to a human dick—spanned twice as far down its shaft. Alec had to admit, it was a bold looking cock.

Miros rumbled another chuckle. "You forget to listen."

Alec quickly turned and closed his eyes. So busted. But sure enough, the sound of Miros' gently pattering stream got his own junk to finally cooperate. Granted, it did nothing to help his boner, but at least his bladder was emptying. Alec groaned at the glorious, merciful sensation, halfway tempted to thank Miros for his help. If only his nuts would climb on board and get with the program, too.

Long moments later, he gingerly shook his dick, then winced as he crammed it awkwardly away. Still super-sensitive. Still super-hard.

Miros watched him, lips curved, back to leaning against a tree with his big arms folded across his chest. "You like my cock."

Alec stilled. "I do not."

"You were staring at it longingly."

"I was staring at it because it's huge."

"Indeed. But also because you want it."

Alec scoffed and started walking. "In your dreams."

Miros chuckled softly. "And your future."

Alec shot him a look as he stalked back to camp, but refused to give a reply. Their conversation was freaking him out, in more ways than he cared to admit. Miros just smiled and gave his leash a playful tug.

As soon as they arrived, Miros returned him to his tree, securing his leash to a thick branch overhead. Roni handed Alec a water bottle as Miros headed to Chet next. Alec eyed Gesh's pack as they milled about, some still rummaging through the team's sacks. Others were eating or engaged in conversation. And not just with each other. A couple were actually shooting it with the scientists, who surprisingly, didn't appear to mind. Weren't they pissed that they were being held captive? Guess their drive to discover all things new trumped every other emotion.

Alec looked to where Zaden was still tied to his post, sitting super still with eyes closed.

"Psst. Yo, Zaden."

Zaden stirred and looked his way.

"You doing okay?"

Z shifted with a wince and gave a shrug. "Not dead, so yeah, I guess."

Alec moved as close as his lead would let him and sat down next to his friend. "We gotta make a plan. Have you seen where they put our weapons?"

Zaden shook his head, his features tight.

"Shit." Alec glanced around. "Seen any weapons of theirs?"

A small nod. "Yeah. They've each got some knives. And obviously they've got tranq darts."

Alec pursed his lips. "What they hit us with yesterday."

Another curt nod. Another pained face. "Too bad they waited till *after* we ate."

"Fuck. Don't remind me."

"Like you weren't already thinking about it."

Alec looked at Z. "You know about the fruit?"

"Yeah. Did the math. But Naydo over there confirmed it." Zaden gestured with his chin to a Kríe by the fire. "That big fucker, going through my shit."

Alec eyed the male. "They're *all* big fuckers."

A groan escaped Zaden's lips, the sound laced with a need for sex. So much so, that it instantly made Alec have to adjust his junk. Though, truth be told, he was kind of afraid to touch it.

Ultimately, he couldn't resist.

Grinding the heel of his palm into his fly, he grimaced through a curse. "Gesh told me this shit won't go away on its own. Miros said something similar, too. God, I really hope they're lying."

Zaden moaned again, but louder. "If they're not, we're fucking screwed."

Alec wondered if he'd meant that literally or figuratively. Scratch that. He didn't want to know.

Miros returned with Chet, securing him on the other side of the campfire, and came to collect Zaden next. Z winced with a grunt as he got to his feet, hobbling off to take his turn. Alec watched him go, then looked at Chet and sighed. So much for planning an escape before they left.

Before long, the science trio had taken a piss, too, and now Gesh's pack readied to go. Each draped a black strap across his chest loaded with blades and other items. Then, while six shouldered on the team's backpacks, another secured Alec's team to one long rope. Single file. Attached by their collars.

But they were also tied individually, too, in a way that made Alec's belly churn with dread. Because even though their wrists were bound in front of their bodies, they were also connected to a rope between their legs. One that continuously grazed their nuts as it ran up their spines to their collars. With very little slack, it essentially made any arm movement a risk to the family jewels. Which didn't just make escape a lot more difficult, but ensured constant contact with their junk; hands unavoidably bumping their cocks while trying to keep that rope from rubbing their balls.

And Alec thought the night had been long.

CHAPTER FIVE

* * *

After a few hours of hiking, Gesh's pack finally stopped, parking it by a large, flowing river. And it was a damn good thing, too, because Alec and his teammates had had nearly all they could stand. Yeah, they were dying of fricking thirst, and could use something to fill their bellies, but most of all they needed a serious breather from all the genital stimulation.

The first hour had been bearable. Barely, but still. The second had been way more uncomfortable. The third hour, however, was when Alec began to suspect that things were going to get ugly. At which point, he stopped hoping that the fruit would wear off, and began fearing the ultimate worst. That the longer that sex mojo stayed in their systems, the worse its effects would become. Because it wasn't just his dick and nuts going crazy anymore, but holy shit, his asshole, too. It'd grown so sensitive, so needy for friction, that every single time he took a step it was all he could do not to drop.

Jaw clenched, hands fisted, he sank to his knees the second their leash holder stopped. And what do you know, his team went tumbling at damn near the exact same time.

"Oh, God," Jamis strained out. "I can't. I can't do it."

Beside him, Zaden grimaced and clutched his junk.

"Just… need to rest," Chet grunted. "That's all. Soon we'll feel better. We've got to."

Bailey groaned in frustration. "I don't wanna feel better *soon*. I need to feel better *now*."

Noah turned to Alec, all but panting. "Gesh said… he told you… how to make… this stop."

Alec winced and shook his head. "You don't want to know."

"Yes, I do."

"No. Trust me. You don't."

Chet eyed him angrily. "That's not your call. We have a fucking right to know."

Alec cursed, squeezing his cock to the point of pain. "Fine. He said it wouldn't stop until we actually came."

"Ah, God," Bailey groused. "I can't. I tried."

"Shit," Zaden ground out. "I did, too."

"I think it's safe to say we all tried," Alec muttered. "But apparently we need a partner."

His teammates went silent. Just stared at him warily.

"You mean," Jamis finally dared to clarify. "We need to actually *fuck* someone to come?"

"Maybe?" Alec answered. "I think? I dunno. I don't really understand myself."

"For fuck's sake," Chet snarled. "You better be wrong, since all we got around here are guys."

Gesh strode over with an armful of fruit. "Tukah?" *Hungry?* He eyed them on the ground. "You all look very… depleted."

"We all look very *tortured*," Chet snapped. "You perv. I should kick your ass for pulling this stunt."

Gesh grinned and dumped his melons on the ground. "I believe Roni has called first dibs on a skirmish."

Chet glowered. "You tell him to bring it on. Any fucking time. Any day."

Gesh inclined his head and sat down next to Noah, motioning for him to enjoy the fresh food. Noah eyed the stuff dubiously. "Thanks, but no thanks. Got a new aversion to fruit."

Gesh chuckled and leaned back against a tree. "These will do nothing but give you strength."

"I think we'd rather starve," Alec muttered dryly, trying to ignore his tingling ass. "Hopefully we'll get lucky and pass out from low blood sugar."

Gesh regarded them for a minute, then called to Naydo, ordering him to bring them their rations. "En reesa." *And water*, he tacked on, too, as the big male headed for their packs.

Noah cleared his throat and looked at Gesh. "Is it true what Alec said? That we're gonna have to fuck someone to get this shit to stop?"

Gesh glanced at Alec with a puzzled look. "No. He misunderstood."

Alec eyed him irritably. "Then by all means, explain."

Gesh shrugged and stretched out his long, dark legs. "You do not need to fuck another, but you *do* need another to fuck *you*."

Alec's whole team stopped breathing, including Alec.

"So, we *don't* need to come?" Jamis looked confused.

"No." Gesh shook his head. "You definitely *must*. It is the only way to find relief."

Again, the team swapped baffled expressions.

Gash studied them curiously, his brows drawing together. "Do you not have plants like senna`sohnsay on Earth? A fruit where, once eaten, one cannot spill seed until they themselves are filled with seed, too?"

"Uh… Yeah, no." Bailey shook his head. "We definitely don't have anything like that."

Noah frowned. "I don't understand the point of such a plant."

Gesh shrugged. "We believe it is Nira's way of ensuring we procreate. Eating her fruit makes the act more intentional. More deliberate. And the outcome more successful."

Everyone's perplexed looks quickly deepened.

"Procreate?" Jamis repeated. "With another male?"

Gesh eyed them more intently, his brows furrowing closer. "Does human life not start with the mixing of seed?"

Noah shook his head. "Uh…No. Not exactly. But I'd love to hear how that works."

Gesh exhaled as if he didn't particularly want to go into it. "After a male eats of Nira's fruit, he soon requires another male to fill him with seed. That seed breaches his inner jewel where senna`sohnsay has made it permeable. Their two sccds mix, which triggers release, and if procreation is their will, they then take their seed to Nira's womb." Gesh glanced at each man. "Is that not the way of your kind?"

They all stared just at him.

Finally, Noah answered. "Um. No. We need a man and a *woman* to reproduce. Our, uh, seed mixes with her egg."

"A *woman?*" Again, Gesh seemed mystified, as he had when Alec had spoken of women earlier. Ultimately, though, he let loose a laugh. "That certainly is not the way of things here. Perhaps your bodies are adapting."

Bailey frowned. "Why would our biology work differently here?"

A second time, Gesh shrugged as he swiped up a fruit. "Maybe the air here, the water, the food, have affected your fundamental functions."

Alec stilled at the thought. Was that even possible?

Chet grimaced and rubbed his fly. "Well that's just great. What the fuck are we gonna do now?"

Gesh looked at him oddly. "The answer is simple. Force yourselves to suffer, or spill."

Chet glared at him, but didn't reply.

Zaden asked the next question. "So, if some of us could still come, hadn't eaten the fruit, we could fix each other without Kríe help?"

Gesh canted his head thoughtfully. "I suppose it is possible." His lips curved into another smirk. "Perhaps one day you should try and find out."

Beside him, Noah eyed Gesh's imposing frame. "It'd definitely make for a better fit."

Gesh met his gaze. His dark eyes hooded. "Oh, meesha. You and I, we would fit together fine."

Noah blinked, then quickly cleared his throat. "Don't think that's even physically possible."

Gesh idly fingered Noah's small, blond ponytail. "I assure you, little beauty, it is."

Alec and the others watched them curiously. They had this strange yet intriguing dynamic going on. Like some subtle, underlying magnetic pull. Come to think of it, it'd been there from the start, when Gesh first caught sight of Noah's face. That lingering stare, and all the others that followed, including the ones Noah returned. They both just seemed to always migrate subconsciously to the other one's side.

Alec looked at Noah. He knew the guy was gay. He'd always been pretty open about it. And of course, as a scientist, he was open-minded, too. But just how far did his open-mindedness go?

Naydo arrived with one of their backpacks and promptly began dumping out its contents. Food rations and water bottles spilled to the ground, along with a bunch of other supplies.

Gesh released Noah's hair, gave his earlobe a little stroke, then rose back onto his feet. "Eat your food. We continue on our way soon." He looked at Naydo, who'd sat down next to Zaden. "Let them wade in the river when they've finished. Perhaps that will ease them for a while."

Naydo nodded, watching Zaden snag up a package and rip it open. Zaden regarded him in return as he took a bite. The two just stared until Naydo emitted a pleased rumble and leaned back against a tree. Guess he'd be hanging out until they were done. Alec studied him as they ate, not that anyone ate much. Just a few bites in and suddenly the team seemed oddly, and suspiciously, full. Like the stuff no longer agreed with their stomachs.

Noting that everyone had finished eating, Naydo gave their leash a tug and gestured to the river. "Nenya. Reesa feyah. Bukah kai." *Come. Cold water. Very pleasing.*

Bailey was the first to lurch to his feet. "Cold fucking water. I'm down with that."

Alec stood, too, because he'd have to agree. It definitely sounded refreshing.

The rest followed suit and headed over with Naydo to where crystalline waters awaited them. But as Naydo untied their wrists so they could strip, Chet abruptly stopped moving completely. "Nothing in that water's gonna attack us, right?"

Naydo scanned the teal depths with a contemplative expression, then shook his head and unfastened his kilt. "No. You should be safe, but I will accompany you as precaution."

The team swapped tentative looks, but ultimately their misery won out. Wrists rebound and bodies naked, they waded into the water, soft sighs quickly spilling free. It wasn't total relief, not by a long shot, but any reprieve at all was priceless. Alec moaned as coolness engulfed his junk and eased the needy burn in his ass. God, if only they could stay there forever.

Deeper they descended, then deeper still, until water lapped at their rock-hard nipples. Alec shivered at the feeling. Until now, he hadn't realized just how fevered he'd been. So good... Aw, yeah. So good...

Naydo brought them to a stop and let them linger. More happy moans, because truth be told, any walking at all was still jarring. Yeah, because of the rope that kept grazing Alec's nuts, but especially because of his teeming back door.

Not caring about anything but finding relief, he reached between his legs past his balls. Restlessly, he rubbed at his sensitized hole. Gave it what it wanted. *Fucking friction.* His eyes rolled back at the potent sensation, savoring the feel of his touch.

Yeah... Back and forth... Just like that....

Shit, now it needed penetration. Needed him to breach its tight little muscle and shove a finger inside. Next thing Alec knew, he was spreading his stance and doing exactly that. Ah! Ah, shit! He anxiously pumped, then grimaced in tortured bliss. Because one, he couldn't seem to reach deep enough, and two, his finger felt way too small. Fortunately, the latter was a pretty easy fix. He sank in a second, and then a third, wincing in raw pleasure as he stretched. Fuck, that hurt, but felt so damn good.

Around him, the similar sounds of his teammates faded as Miros' voice filled his head. Specifically, the words he'd murmured that morning about how his dick was in Alec's future— which Alec presumed meant up his ass. But in this moment, he wanted nothing more. Because without a doubt, Miros could definitely reach deep enough, and could definitely spread him good.

All but delirious, Alec tried to shove deeper, but jerked when he hit something swollen. Swollen and unbelievably sensitive. Inhaling sharply, he yanked his fingers free, eyes snapping wide in surprise. Despite how fucking good that felt, he instinctively knew he couldn't afford to go there. He'd learned his lesson the night before while watching Gesh and Roni get freaky. Too much stimulation equaled wicked discomfort. No way was he risking that again.

He glanced around, finding his teammates' eyes closed, their tense brows scrunched tightly together. And just like his had been, their arms were flexing, as if busy working things down below. Shit, maybe someone would actually get lucky.

Alec's gaze moved to Zaden, who stood the closest. His head had fallen back and his shoulders were bunching from whatever he was doing to his junk. Curious thing, though, was how he was inching subconsciously closer to Naydo. And fuck if Naydo didn't look pleased. Turning to face him, Naydo waited as Z approached, his golden eyes straight-up smoldering.

Alec couldn't look away, couldn't keep from watching, as Z absently drifted closer. Slowly, Naydo closed his big arms around him, making sure not to let their bodies touch. Then, ever so carefully, he dipped his head and breathed against Zaden's neck. Eyes still shut, Zaden shivered with a moan, his breaths turning instantly shallow. Naydo's full lips curved. Zaden's biceps bunched faster, his brows pinched tight in desperation.

Alec's heart pounded. God, they were less than an inch apart, but Zaden was too out of it to know. Alec should tell him, he knew he should, but he just couldn't get his mouth moving. Besides that, he also had a curious feeling that Naydo's intentions weren't bad. That on some level, the big Kríe was merely captivated. Drawn in some way to Zaden's energy.

Again, Naydo exhaled against Z's skin. And again, Z shuddered in response.

Fucking hell. How could such a simple act look so effing erotic? Alec inched away from their two-person inferno.

But then Naydo lifted his hand from the water and bit off the tips of his first two claws. Alec frowned in confusion, but quickly understood when Naydo sank said hand down toward Z's ass. All while taking painstaking care not to let their bodies touch. Probably because he knew that if he did, Zaden would snap to awareness.

Two seconds later, though, Naydo no longer seemed concerned. Boldly, he brushed his lips to Z's ear as his lowered arm's muscles *contracted*. Looked like Naydo's fingers just made swift, direct contact to a very specific place.

Zaden jerked with a gasp, but his eyes stayed closed as he fell forward into Naydo's chest. The huge male purred and pulled him closer. And then, as his free arm held Z in place, his other arm started steadily flexing. Presumably doing only God knew what to Z's ass with those long, de-clawed fingers. Well, actually, Alec had a pretty good idea, considering the way his friend was suddenly writhing.

Alec cursed, knowing full well he should snap Zaden out of it, but shit, the expression Z was wearing looked so blissful. So filled with a pleasure like nothing else, that Alec just couldn't make himself do it. Naydo wasn't hurting Z. He was easing his pain. Or if nothing else, distracting him from his torment.

Again, Alec gripped his own rigid cock, enviously looking on. Watching as his co-pilot twitched and squirmed, rapturously trapped in Naydo's arms. Alec's asshole clenched, imagining the pleasure. Zaden's features pinched tighter. His muffled moans quickened. Did Naydo have one finger inside him or two? Abruptly, Zaden jerked with a stifled grunt. Definitely had two inside him now.

Tiny waves lapped against their fevered bodies as Z pressed his face into Naydo's chest. Naydo made a husky sound and flexed his biceps faster. Zaden grimaced in ecstasy, mouth falling open. But then he abruptly groaned in pain and bit Naydo's beefy pec. Alec cringed, knowing why. Z was peaking but couldn't come. As if understanding, too, Naydo growled super low and hefted Zaden higher up his body. Alec's eyes shot wide. Oh, fuck. Oh, God. Naydo was going to impale Z on his—

"Whoa! Holy shit!" Bailey barked to Alec's right. "Something just grabbed my ankle!"

Zaden snapped to awareness, then jerked in alarm, finding himself caged in Naydo's arms. Naydo snarled, clearly frustrated, but let him go to turn and scan the waters.

Distracted by the sudden threat of danger, Alec nervously searched his surroundings. Not that he knew what he was looking for. Naydo did, though. Alec could tell by his expression. And the Kríe did *not* look happy.

Great.

Clearing his throat, Alec continued to look around. "Uh, correct me if I'm wrong, Naydo, but you suddenly look concerned. Please tell me your rivers don't have piranha."

Naydo paused to frown at him. "Piranha?"

Alec nodded. "Flesh-eating water creatures that travel in large numbers?"

Naydo grunted with a nod. "Ah, yes. We have those. But that is not what I search for."

Alec swapped disturbed looks with Zaden and the others. Because, honestly, what the fuck could be worse than piranha? His heart sank as more possibilities came to mind. Alligators. Anacondas. Leeches. Eels. Suddenly, their river break didn't seem all that smart.

"Then what exactly *are* you searching for?"

"Oonmaiyos," Naydo muttered, starting them toward shore, his eyes still scanning intently.

"Oon-what-ohs?" Bailey frowned. "What the fuck are those?"

"Water nomads."

Chet scoffed. "What, like half man, half fish?"

"Yes. And a species with whom we do not get along."

Bailey's eyes went wide as they reached the bank. Then a huge smile spread across his face. "Holy son of a wombat-crazed whore. A merman just touched my leg."

The science trio instantly fell into conversation, while Alec, Chet, and Z looked less enthused. But as they reached their clothes and started dressing, Roni's warning bellow seized their full attention.

"Bellacoy! Tacha! Aussa shawní!" *Flyers! Quickly! Into the trees!*

Immediately, every male dropped whatever he was doing and scaled the nearest stalk. Naydo, however, stayed with Alec's team, ushering them away from the river.

"What's going on?" Jamis blurted, nearly tripping.

Naydo grinned as he gestured them behind a tall bush. "Watch, little one, and see." With deft agility, he climbed the trunk beside them and quickly tied their leash out of reach.

Jamis craned his head back, calling up to him with a frown. "But—"

"Stay here. Be quiet. And do not let them see you." And just like that, Naydo was off to join his pack, moving like a wraith through the trees.

A few seconds later, Alec heard the grating shriek of something big back at the river. His eyes shot wide when the creatures dropped into view. They were the same three dragons—or at least the same kind—that attacked their ship and caused them to crash.

"Son of a bitch," Zaden murmured in awe. "Those fuckers are even bigger than I remember."

Chet whistled low. "Look at the size of their jaws."

Noah shook his head. "Look at the size of their *wings*. No wonder they didn't follow us into the trees. They'd never have the space to lift back off."

The beasts touched down at the water's edge where a few Kríe stood as bait. Patiently, methodically, they lured the flyers in, away from the open river into tree cover. The huge creatures lunged, jaws snapping at the Kríe's heads. But before they could let loose another mighty squawk, the rest of Gesh's pack descended. With perfect precision, they dove from the treetops, landing atop the flyers' broad backs. The beasts reared back, but the males clung tight, even as taloned wings sliced their flesh. So fiercely focused. So deadly determined.

Captivated, Alec watched as the pack worked as one. Plunging daggers deep for makeshift anchors while shrewdly slashing every strategic location. Wing junctures, leg tendons, up under the ribs. Buying time until a Kríe reached their throats. The flyers thrashed and screeched. Their jugulars spewed, showering everything around them in blood.

The scene was incredible. Ferocious. Intense. Not to mention horrific and grisly. One thing was for sure, though. After this display of primal dominance, had Alec not already been sporting a boner, he definitely would've had one now.

Lasting a total of maybe five minutes, the takedown was over like that. Victory roars and celebratory howls tore through every inch of the forest. So bad, Alec wanted to go over and get a look.

But Chet's curt snarl quickly yanked him back to reality. "Show's over, guys. Help me find something to cut this rope."

The whole team snapped to attention fast.

"Those might work." Jamis pointed beneath a shrub.

Nice. Rock shards. And a lot of them, too. The guys snatched them up and got busy sawing, even as their minds kept on reeling.

"Man," Bailey murmured. "That was some crazy shit."

Noah shook his head. "Dragons… Unreal."

Zaden frowned over his shoulder. "Makes you wonder if there's anything that Kríe pack *can't* hunt."

Alec slid him a look, knowing exactly what Z meant. Even if they *did* manage to cut their leash in time, would they really be able to evade Gesh for long? It didn't take a rocket scientist to deduce the answer to that one.

Chet scowled, clearly coming to the same conclusion, and sped up the pace of his sawing. "We gotta fucking try. I refuse to just give up."

He was right and Alec knew it. Hell, everyone did. Taking his lead, they all worked faster, steadily severing the fibers of their rope.

Jamis glanced toward the river. "They're completely preoccupied. We should definitely have time to—"

"What are you doing?" came a velvety purr from above.

Alec froze, then discreetly shoved the shard into his pocket.

"Goddamn it!" Chet threw his to the ground.

Naydo's chuckle descended like a warm, weighted blanket. "Do not fret. Had you not tried, I would have thought less of you for it. Perhaps next time I will let you run free, let you frolic a bit before rounding you up."

"Fuck you," Chet bit out. "You big purple dick."

Naydo threw back his head and laughed some more.

Alec sighed. "Chet, seriously. Don't encourage him."

Beside him, the trio's lips twitched.

Zaden, however, watched Naydo intently as he untied their rope and jumped down. There was a look in his eyes that Alec couldn't quite place. But considering who he was looking at, Alec suspected it had something to do with Naydo—and what those two did during the team's little swim. Alec still didn't know what to make of that, but hadn't really had a chance to mull it over yet. So it wouldn't surprise him if Zaden was presently trying to wrap his brain around it, too.

CHAPTER SIX

* * *

Led back to the others, Alec finally got his eyeful. Talk about a massacre. The three dragons lay motionless, covered in blood, as a handful of Kríe skinned and sectioned them.

"You eat *flyer* meat?" Bailey asked Naydo as he stared at the carnage.

"Mah." *No.* A voice that *wasn't* Naydo's. But a voice Alec recognized all the same. He turned in its direction as Miros arrived, Roni coming to a stop by his side. "We do not eat meat, but we do trade and sell it."

Jamis coughed in surprise. "You don't eat meat?" Incredulously, he eyed Miros' bulky frame. "Then how the hell do you stay so big?"

Miros shrugged, his gaze flicking over to Alec. "We find what we need in other things."

Alec shifted under his stare, then noticed his bleeding arm. Looked like a flyer got him good.

Naydo lifted his chin to Miros and Roni. "Does Gesh want to take all that meat to the homeland?"

Roni nodded. "Yes, but preparing it for transport will take some time and Gesh does not want to wait. Some will stay behind and meet up with us later."

"What's the hurry?" Chet muttered.

Roni slid him a smirk. "Gesh is anxious to sell his *other* wares." Slowly, his gaze roamed down Chet's body. "Wares I will certainly miss."

The whole team immediately stilled at his words.

"He's going to fucking *sell* us?" Alec bit out in disbelief.

Roni shrugged. "Or give you as gifts."

The science trio paled.

"Give us as *gifts?*" Chet balled his fists. "Over my dead body."

"To be given as gifts is the highest compliment, especially when gifted to our king."

Holy what the fuck?

Alec's eyes shot to Zaden, who looked equally floored.

Roni smiled and rubbed Chet's skull-cut head. "Do not worry. You and I, we will still have our fun."

Chet seethed and shoved his hand away, then flat-out lunged at the male. "Don't you fucking touch me," he barked, his bound hands gunning for Roni's throat. "Or, swear to God, I'll—"

Roni dodged and slammed Chet's back into a tree. Alec and the team stumbled with them. Hello, still attached to the same lead! But neither Chet nor Roni seemed to notice as Roni pinned Chet's body with his own.

"Or you swear you will do what?" Roni purred super smug.

"Untie me, bitch, and I'll show you."

Roni chuffed in amusement and licked Chet's cheek. "For some reason I like when you call me bitch. Soon I will call you the same." Stepping back abruptly, he removed Chet's collar, then glanced at Alec as he untied Chet's hands. "I am going to help your friend release some tension. Do not worry. I promise not to kill him."

Alec stiffened. "Uh, yeah, thanks, but I don't think so. The size difference is—"

"Boss," Chet grit out, eyes flashing fire. "For the love of God, let me fucking do this."

Alec shouldn't have been surprised. Chet was practically part Pitbull. One of the reasons Alec hired him on. But he couldn't afford to risk the guy getting injured. Chet was vital to the team's survival.

"Chet," he chuckled tensely. "Come on, man. You're angry. And clearly not thinking straight." He gestured to Roni. "He's freaking huge. No way you could—"

"*Please*," Chet persisted. "He's been nothing but a punk. Gimme a chance to put him on his ass."

Roni crossed his arms and smiled at Alec. "You are smart. Understand that your kind is inferior. At least one in your unit shows intelligence."

Alec's blood boiled at the insult. But even though he knew Roni was blatantly goading him, he couldn't tamp back human pride. Eyes narrowing, he gave Chet a single nod. "Have fun," he muttered. "Don't make me regret this."

"Yes," Chet hissed, his excitement palpable.

A sly grin spread across Roni's face. "Bellah. Nenya." *Good. Come.* He led them to an open space.

As Alec's team looked on, Gesh and some others came to watch, too. Honest to God, if Chet wound up dead, Alec was going to fucking kill him.

Slowly, the two males began to circle, eyeing each other intently.

Roni raked another hot gaze down Chet's body. "Will you give me a prize, warrior, if I win this exchange?"

"Sure. But if I win, I want the same deal."

Roni's fangs flashed wickedly. "Agreed. Name your prize."

"Alright… If I win, no more tying me up."

Roni's lips curved. "I accept. If you win, no more ropes. But if I win, you must fully submit."

Chet's brows furrowed warily. "Fully submit how?"

"By becoming my plaything. My bitch."

Chet paled and glanced at Alec.

Alec groaned and shook his head. Roni just played them like a goddamn fiddle. No way would Chet's pride let him fold.

Roni came to a stop and pompously smiled, giving a big beefy shrug. "If you are scared, it is not too late to change your mind."

Chet bristled. "Fuck you, Roni. I don't back down." Without warning, he rushed him, plowing his shoulder into Roni's gut, his arms snapping tight around Roni's waist. At six foot three and two hundred and twenty pounds, that was definitely no lightweight hit.

Roni grunted, stumbling back, and damn near falling, as he tried to grab hold of Chet, too. But Chet just kept charging, boots chewing up the ground, until he slammed Roni into a tree.

Alec grinned. Gesh laughed.

Roni coughed up a chuckle, too. "Bellah kai, kensa. Reeka moonsah may." *Very nice, warrior. Give me more of that.*

Chet glared as he pinned him, but before he could reply, Roni hefted him up and head-butted him in the face.

Alec cringed as the rest of his team winced in sympathy. Chet had to be seeing stars.

Cursing through a groan, Chet palmed his eye as Roni marched them from the tree and slammed him. Right on his back atop the unforgiving ground. Air punched from Chet's lungs, but he was far from defeated. Roni loomed above him all arrogant and superior. Chet glowered and lurched to his feet.

"More?" Roni grinned.

"More," Chet growled.

Again, Chet lunged with the exact same move. But when Roni anticipated and tried to dodge, Chet anticipated, too, and nailed him. This time, however, when Chet shoulder-rammed Roni's midsection, he aimed the hit slightly further down. Enough that he could grab the backs of Roni's knees and yank the things forward until they buckled.

Roni grunted as his back slammed hard into the ground.

Tackle!

Alec's eyebrows shot high. Well, look at that. Though he probably shouldn't be too surprised. Chet *had* played offensive lineman in college. The science trio whooped, blatantly jazzed, as across the way, Gesh and company smirked. Alec frowned at their expressions, but was quickly distracted when Chet scrambled up and sat on Roni's body. Muscular thighs straddling the huge Kríe's lean waist, Chet hauled back and clocked him in the face.

Roni stilled, then slowly grinned wicked wide. As if the pain Chet just inflicted turned him on. Chet snarled, cocked his elbow, and threw another punch. But this time Roni deflected Chet's fist with his forearm and nailed Chet with a "snake strike" to his sternum.

Chet grunted, then grimaced and wheezed for breath. But that brief pause would be the beginning of the end. Roni's big hand slammed the side of his face, sending him sprawling to the ground. And just like that, Roni was on top of Chet, pinning him flat on his back. Noses nearly touching, the Kríe bared his fangs. "Tah, Chet." *Yes.* "Your anger excites me."

Chet cursed and tried to shove him off, but his efforts were hopelessly futile. Roni outweighed him by a good hundred pounds. Adding insult to injury, the Kríe reached between their bodies and cupped Chet's tender nuts. Chet gasped. Alec cringed, knowing that couldn't feel good. Didn't matter that Roni wasn't even squeezing.

Roni chuckled and grazed his fangs down Chet's throat. Chet froze, then thrashed harder to get away. To Alec's surprise, Roni actually let him go. Well, sort of. The second he lifted up and Chet rolled out from under him, Roni shoved him back to the ground on his chest. And this time he didn't let Chet off the hook so easy. Grabbing his wrist, Roni twisted Chet's arm and pinned the thing painfully against Chet's spine.

"Ah!" Chet howled. "Goddamn it! Aw, fuck!"

Roni grinned and settled his body atop Chet's, then ground his dick against Chet's ass. A dick that was undoubtedly rock hard. "Do you yield?" he murmured, lips brushing Chet's ear.

Features tight, Chet panted. "No way."

Roni rumbled happily and licked Chet's neck. "Good. I am so very glad to hear it."

Using his own knees to spread Chet's wider, Roni wedged his cock even deeper between Chet's cheeks. Evidently his fun wouldn't be deterred by Chet's shorts. Chet cursed. Then stifled a needy moan.

Roni grinned and nuzzled the side of his neck. "You want my cock."

Chet coughed. "In your purple fucking dreams."

"Oh, no," Roni chuckled. "Not in my dreams. In your tight little warrior ass."

"Fuck you," Chet bit out.

"I would rather fuck you." Roni rocked his hips, slow and steady. "I think you would rather that, too."

Another restless moan escaped Chet's lips as his eyes rolled back into his head. Roni nuzzled him again, then nudged Chet's wrist higher.

Chet's eyes flew back open. "Ah, shit! Motherfuck!"

"Do you yield?" Roni repeated, biting Chet's ear.

Chet's brows pinched furiously, his mind clearly at odds. "No," he grated. "I don't fucking yield."

Again, Roni chuckled. "Very well, when you are ready. But you will have to say the word. I will not be asking again."

"Yeah?" Chet rasped. "And why is that?"

"Because," Roni purred. "From here on out my mouth will be very busy."

And that was the only heads up that Chet got.

Roni sank his sharp fangs between Chet's shoulder and neck.

Chet gasped, eyes wide, every muscle going stiff. That is, until Roni started to suck. Once he did, holy freaking hell. Chet's hips started thrusting like mad.

"Fuck!" he panted. "Aw, shit! Aw, fuck!"

Seemed Roni's fangs were some potent little bastards. Chet fisted and clawed at the damp, lush ground as his eyes kept rolling back in his head.

Alec swapped uneasy looks with Zaden. Roni said he wouldn't kill him, and Chet's predicament didn't look fatal. But what if Roni was sucking him dry or something, while everyone just stood around watching? No fucking way would Alec let that happen. Whether the stubborn fucker yielded or not.

Stepping forward, he readied to open his mouth, but Miros appeared and quickly intercepted.

"He is not in any danger. I assure you, he is fine. Kríe bites are very common practice."

"But—"

"Trust me." Miros slid him a roughish smile. "Chet will be yielding any moment."

Alec frowned and looked back at the team's pinned bodyguard. Face flushed, Chet was still trying to fuck the ground as Roni suckled and dry humped him from above. But just like Miros said, when Roni sank his fangs deeper, Chet arched in a howl of surrender.

"Ah! Okay! Goddamn it! I yield!"

Gesh's pack raised their fists.

Chet's team bit back groans.

And Roni loosed a long, happy growl.

Gently, he eased his teeth from Chet's neck and lazily lapped at the wounds. "Such a good little bitch. Tonight you will submit, and lead the way for your team."

"The way?" Chet groaned.

Roni grinned. "Indeed. To show them they have nothing to fear."

"Nothing," Chet repeated. "You sure about that?"

"Well… Nothing and absolutely everything."

* * *

With festivities over and everyone patched up—compliments of the team's first aid kits—the caravan was back on its way. Chet, however, stayed pretty quiet for the journey. And honestly, Alec was grateful for that. The guy's predicament was uncomfortable to think about. Almost as uncomfortable as the fucking rope dragging back and forth across Alec's balls. God, they were getting so engorged and heavy. If they—or his dick—filled any fuller, Alec feared something was going to split.

Yeah. Awesome visual.

Muscles tense, he ambled next to Zaden, since their leash lent a couple of yards between each prisoner. But Zaden wasn't talking much either. By the grim look on his face, the guy was busy working shit out. Maybe like what happened between him and Naydo. Man, that shit was crazy. And hot.

Alec groaned up at the trees. He must be getting delirious. After all, they hadn't really eaten much and this non-stop bodily torment was exhausting. And then there were the mental aspects. Every tree they passed—and being in the jungle, there were a lot—Alec sized up as a worthy object to grind against. And those huge-ass flowers? With their long, fat pollen tubes? He fantasized shoving those up his ass. Maybe a couple at once, in one big bundle. Which was such a foreign feeling to him. Never had he wanted things crammed up his rectum. But now he yearned for it even more than he yearned for a hot, wet hole to shove his dick in.

So messed up, and yet, that was his reality.

His other messed up reality was how he kept checking out Gesh's pack, like a horny dude ogling chicks. Scrutinizing their bodies from head to toe, lingering on the parts he liked best. Like their broad, bulging shoulder blades. And that ravine down their spines. Or how their abs looked like literal washboards. He especially liked their golden eyes, their wicked smiles, and tiny, pierced nipples. Or how their long dreads swept across their backs every single time they moved. Shit, in all honesty, the list could go on. Everything about them fascinated him.

Which, again, he realized was totally messed up. Because instead of captivating, he should find them vile, for all kinds of sordid reasons. The stunt Gesh pulled with that fruit, for one, of which Alec's team was still suffering. For taking them captive. Treating them like pets. And planning to sell them for profit. His teeth clenched angrily. They were self-serving scoundrels… whom Alec found utterly engrossing.

He cursed under his breath. He knew what was happening. It really was pretty clear. His debilitating need to come had his mind playing tricks on him. Making the things that his body needed look overly attractive and appealing.

He knew it was true, but couldn't do a damn thing about it. His eyes slid back to Miros, walking up ahead, who had all but offered Alec his dick. Now Alec wanted to take him up on that. Not that he ever would. Because, honestly, no matter how the dice rolled, their parts just weren't compatible. Miros was too big. Straight-up. End of. Simple unfortunate fact. Which in itself made Alec feel kind of queasy. Because with his team unable to find release alone, and Gesh's pack too large to do the job, how in the hell were they going to get fixed?

His mind churned anxiously. Ugh. He needed to stop thinking.

Raw, potent pleasure blazed through his junk and shimmied into his sensitized ass. Alec hissed and looked down, finding that yet again he'd been feverishly stroking his crotch.

Zaden turned at the sound, then frowned dejectedly. "I can't take this much longer, Alec." He shook his head. "I'm seriously gonna lose my mind."

Alec winced as he ground his palm down his length. "I know. It's getting worse. Everything below the belt…" He groaned and forced his hand away. "I can't even think straight anymore."

"Yeah," Zaden muttered, eyes locking on something ahead. "Got one thing on the brain and not much else. I feel like a sex-deranged whore."

Alec followed Z's gaze to exactly what he'd suspected. Or more specifically, *who*. Naydo. The male striding casually beside the trio and two other Kríe who looked like twins. *Identical* twins, down to their piercings. They were a bit smaller, though, and appeared younger, too. Made Alec wonder how old any of them were.

Naydo glanced over his shoulder and met Zaden's gaze. Z held it, but eventually looked away.

Alec regarded the two, then figured it was time to finally broach the question.

Wincing a second time as that damn rope grazed his nuts, he turned and looked at his friend. "So, uh, Z... I've been meaning to ask you something... about back when we were wading in that river..." No point in spelling out the awkward any further. Zaden would know exactly what he was asking.

Z flicked him a wary glance. Released a heavy sigh. "You wanna know what the fuck I was thinking."

Alec shrugged. "Or what's going on."

Zaden shook his head. "I... I have no idea. I mean, one minute I was floating in my own little bubble, just letting all that cool water soothe me. God, it felt good. How it eased the burn."

Alec nodded. Their respite had been way too fleeting.

"And then I was like, maybe if I tried again, with all this cool water helping out. Maybe I'd actually be able to do it. Get myself to finally come." His jaw ticked. "Needed to come so damn bad."

Alec scowled. "You say that in past frickin' tense. I need to come so damn bad *now*."

Zaden chuckled darkly, but his smile quickly faded. "So I got to stroking, and suddenly my little bubble consumed everything around me. I couldn't hear you guys. Couldn't see you. Forgot you were even there. All I knew, all my body was comprehending, was my urgent attempt to find release." He shuddered, then immediately shuddered again. "And then all of a sudden, this powerful, sensual presence infiltrated my little bubble. But the presence felt good. I liked it. A lot. Kinda felt like it was aiding my cause. And the sensations got stronger, and the pressure kept building, and then suddenly that presence was everywhere." Wincing, he restlessly rubbed at his bulge. "And then, it wasn't just moving all around me, but sliding inside of me, too. Ah God, Alec," he groaned. "Felt so fucking good. Can't even begin to explain."

Alec squeezed his fly, the vivid scene replaying in his head. "So… even then… you still didn't realize?"

A flush climbed up Z's neck to his cheeks. "I think part of me knew, but didn't care. Just wanted to keep on going. But then, out of nowhere, shit turned *excruciating*..."

"I think Naydo knew and was going to try and help. Shit, I think he was going to fuck you right there."

Zaden shot him an almost sheepish look. "I know. And I would've let him."

Alec cringed. "Ah, God. He would've torn you in half."
"Yeah." Z frowned. "You're probably right. Guess it's a good thing it didn't happen."

CHAPTER SEVEN

* * *

They arrived at camping spot number two just before dusk. Although, it wasn't exactly a camping spot. According to Gesh, it was the pack's main dwelling. How convenient that it was located along the way. Nestled amidst the foliage against the side of a mountain, it looked like some primitive resort.

As their entourage filed in, dumping gear off with happy sighs, Alec eyed the eccentric area. They must've cleared away tons of trees to have such a spread in the middle of the jungle. If he were to guess, he'd say it was roughly the size of an extra-large hockey rink. With some taller trees still intact, its perimeter was lined by the ten-foot stone enclosure they just entered through. Against said enclosure's entire interior, large bushes covered nearly every inch, overflowing with colorful produce. If they yielded that much fruit for even half of the year, these Kríe would never go hungry.

At the center of the encampment was a huge stone fire pit, surrounded by lots of open space. At the far end, a waterfall rained down from tall rock, with a sizeable pool sparkling at its base. On the side from which they'd just entered, though, small boulders and lush plants encircled a steaming spring. God, Alec would gladly take either of those to wash off two days' worth of sweat.

His gaze slid to the structure spanning one side of the compound's length, from one basin of water to the other. Snug against the mountain, the two-story lodging sat wholly exposed on one side. Exposed, as in open. As in no freaking wall for the entire stretch that faced the fire pit. Comprised solely of sleeping units, Alec could literally see each one, side by side, between thick rustic walls. Like a great big cubby shelf stacked two-high. With no visible furniture, but strewn with plush furs, the nooks gave new meaning to cozy.

Alec turned to the trees across the way, on the fire pit's other side. Tall and sturdy, they supported random platforms, the lowest elevated roughly fifteen feet. Alec wondered what they were used for. To watch for intruders? As tree stands for hunting prey? Someone obviously wanted a bird's-eye view of something.

Gesh sauntered over to the team's assigned handlers, gesturing for the twins to approach, too. "Naydo. Miros. Roni. Filli and Finn. Take them to the waterfall and tend to them accordingly." The Kríe inclined their heads, but before Gesh departed, he cut Noah free from the leash. "Come, meesha. I will see to you myself."

Alec frowned as Gesh walked Noah over to the springs, knowing he couldn't do a damn thing to stop him. Not that Noah seemed to mind. Alec's brows furrowed deeper. Come to think of it, by the way Noah was peering up at the male, he kind of looked like he was starting to crush. And not just on the lust-driven level, like Alec and the rest of the team. But in that *other* way, that'd make parting ways tomorrow not very pleasant. Stockholm Syndrome maybe? Who the fuck knew. Was kind of curious what "meesha" meant, though…

They headed past the fire pit and over to the waterfalls, where again, Alec caught himself checking out Miros' ass. That little, black kilt thing just kept snagging his eye. Giving up peek after peek of upper hamstring every time the Kríe took a step. Alec squeezed his cock into submission. Seriously? Lusting after a huge, purple male? God, he was going insane.

Stupid effing fire fruit. He was going to torch that fucking tree.

Miros interrupted his train of thought. "Wash your clothes over there on those rocks, then hang them on the racks by the fire."

Naydo cut them from their leash and motioned toward the waterfall. "Soap is in those baskets. You all stink, so use a lot." A smile played on his lips when Zaden smirked and flipped him off.

Roni grinned and got busy freeing them, too. His task? To separate their wrist binds from the rope that ran between their legs.

Ah, God. Finally. A breather for Alec's nuts.

He moaned in gratitude, not that Roni deserved it, then restlessly rubbed his cock.

Roni untied their hands next so they could pull off their shirts, but then swiftly rebound them back together. Goddamn it. Really? They had to bathe tied up, too?

Ignoring Alec's scowl, Roni turned his eyes to Chet. "Come, my little bitch. We will help each other wash." Chet glowered and didn't move. Roni studied him, then smirked. "Ah. You want another bite."

Aaaaaaand Chet was hustling to the waterfall before Alec could even blink. Roni chuckled and followed after him, undoing his kilt as he went.

Alec turned to Miros, who was getting naked too, minus the bandage on his arm. "Okay, so what's the deal with these "common practice" Kríe bites? Roni's seem to really freak Chet out."

"I do not know why he does not like them. They feel rather good. Very... *stimulating*." Miros set his kilt aside and slid Alec a look. "I would be more than happy to demonstrate, if you like."

Alec's dick throbbed and ass clenched envisioning Miro's mouth on him. Shit, he was halfway tempted to accept. Exhaling raggedly, he looked away. "Uh... Yeah... Thanks. I think I'll pass."

Laundry and shower time went as well as could be expected. It'd been awkward at first, ambling around naked with a raging boner. But after a while he got used to it and relaxed. After all, his team wasn't the only ones doing it. Every single pack mate was, too. Though, why *they* were rock hard, Alec didn't want to know. At least he and his men had an excuse.

Miros breathed against his ear from close behind. "We are aroused because your team smells like needy sex. Like animals in full-blown heat."

Alec froze, half-mortified, half-disconcerted by Miros' stealth. "No way. Are you serious?" He sniffed his pit. Then warily frowned at his junk.

"Yes." Miros chuckled, moving into view. "It is starting to make us crazy." To further illuminate, he tilted his head toward the twins, who were getting pretty friendly with Jamis and Bailey. "I am not sure what they are up to, but they are definitely up to something."

Alec watched the four gesturing and exchanging brief touches. "Um... Should I be worried?"

Miros shook his head. "No. Not worried where they are concerned." Dark eyes glittering, he took a step closer. "But where *you* are concerned, you should definitely be something else."

Alec's stomach churned heatedly. God, Miros was big. With a gaze that was damn near hypnotizing.

"Something else?" he mumbled.

"Tah." Miros nodded. "Hungry, eager, for my cock."

Alec's heart pounded faster. Because he *was* all those things. But for some reason, he just couldn't admit it. God, how he wished Miros would just take the reins, take the responsibility from Alec's hands. The big Kríe wouldn't though. He was going to make Alec man up.

Shit.

Forcing himself to look away, Alec's eyes landed back on the foursome. They'd inched even closer, and their expressions looked more serious. Alec watched as Finn moved to stand at Jamis' back, saw him reach around and grasp Jamis' wrists. But then the Kríe lifted them over Jamis' head and hooked them up around his own nape. Which essentially just trapped Jamis' hands behind Finn's neck, with his backside stretched against the Kríe's front.

Filli promptly followed his lead and did the same to Bailey.

Alec frowned. Why'd his guys just stand there and let them do that? But the lust-fueled heat in both Bailey and Jamis' eyes was pretty much answer enough. As if mimicking a mirror, the twins faced each other and started playing with their captives in unison. Running clawed hands up and down their glistening torsos. Toying with their hard little nipples. Alec's teammates shifted anxiously, abdomens clenching, biceps bunching. But it wasn't until the twins' hands moved lower that the scientists' eyes rolled back in their heads. Lazily, the brothers stroked their rock-hard cocks while nuzzling and lapping at their necks.

Alec blinked. Jamis and Bailey were fucking *blissing*.

"You see?" Miros smiled. "Your men are not worried. They are finally welcoming relief."

Alec's eyes shot back to Miros. "Right fucking here?" Ah, God. Maybe he should, too.

Miros shrugged. "Perhaps. Although, the twins *do* like to play."

Alec wasn't exactly sure what he meant by that. Glancing around, he spotted Zaden with Naydo, standing on the other side of the pool. Chet and Roni, however, were nowhere to be found. Alec wondered if that was good or bad.

Clearing his throat, he pointed to his head. "I, uh, should probably rinse my hair."

He'd literally grabbed a handful of soap from those baskets—smooth stone-like balls slightly smaller than walnuts—and ran them all over his body. Including his nappy head. Surprisingly, the stuff smelled frickin' amazing. Like honeydew and bananas. Actually made him kind of hungry.

Miros accompanied him to the waterfall—guess he had nothing better to do—which proved to be an exercise in pain infliction. Because, yeah, walking normal at this stage in the game wasn't exactly easy. Not when Alec's dick felt like it weighed ten pounds and his nuts felt like they weighed another twenty. All while his asshole screamed bloody murder to be stuffed with something really fucking big. Not that it could handle it. His ass was still a virgin.

Stepping beneath the flow of cool water, Alec rinsed off, then rinsed off again. Felt so damn good to at least be clean. But as he stepped back out, Miros blocked his path, a soap basket held under his bandaged arm.

"Gesh instructed us to tend to your bodies."

Alec frowned as Miros maneuvered them behind the cascade, where the wall of water offered some privacy. Glancing around, he looked back up at Miros. "Uh, I'm pretty sure I washed every inch. Why'd you take me back here?"

Miros smiled and shook his head. "You are not cleansed in every way." He pointed to a raised, slender outcrop in the wall. "Sit."

Alec eyed the thing, but ultimately sat down. Miros set his soap basket down on the ledge, too, then took hold of Alec's bound wrists. Lifting them to a peg mounted in the rock above Alec's head, he hooked them securely in place.

Alec stiffened. "What are you doing?"

Miros sank to his knees. "Readying to cleanse you another way." Without further explanation, he propped Alec's heels on the ledge and spread them the width of his shoulders. Which essentially put Alec's rigid cock right in Miros' face. Apparently, not enough though, because two seconds later, Miros pulled Alec's ass to the edge.

Alec's eyes went wide. "Whoa. I washed there, too. No need to hit it twice."

Miros smiled and pulled the basket closer. "What I am tending to is a bit more extensive."

Grabbing a couple soap rocks, he worked them into a lather, then smoothed the silky suds around Alec's junk. Even along his taint below his nuts. Alec watched him rinse his hands and reach back into the basket to pull out a small, slender blade.

Alec balked. "Oh my God. You're—You're gonna *shave* me?"

"I am," Miros confirmed, swiftly getting busy.

Alec definitely hadn't seen *that* one coming.

Miros removed the hair around Alec's dick, then, slowing down, worked more carefully around his balls. Alec held his breath. That knife looked really sharp. But when Miros moved even lower to Alec's sensitive taint, Alec groaned, fighting like hell not to move.

"Mm. You are swollen here. Try not to rock your hips."

"Yeah," Alec rasped. "Easier said than done."

Gentle scrapes came again and again. Alec's eyes rolled back. Felt so good. But then Miros pulled one cheek to the side and started shaving around his reeling hole. Alec's eyes shot back open. Oh, shit. Way too stimulating.

"Almost done." Miros grazed him with short, light strokes. "You do not have much here to cleanse." A few seconds later, he returned the blade to his basket.

"Done?" Alec exhaled.

"With that part, yes."

"With *that* part? You mean, you have more stuff to do?"

Miros' lips curved. "Yes, but it only involves soap."

Alec frowned. "What more could you possibly wash? I told you, I got fucking everything."

Miros chuckled huskily and fisted Alec's dick. "Where I am washing next, moyo, you never even touched." His other clawed hand eased around Alec's nuts and gently started to fondle.

Alec moaned before he could stop himself. Just felt so damn good. Still, he had no clue what Miros was talking about. He'd definitely cleaned his entire package.

"So heavy." Miros rolled Alec's balls between his fingers. "So heavy and so very full."

Alec swallowed. He should tell him to get off his junk, but damn it, he just couldn't do it. "Trust me. I know," he rasped out instead.

Miros' eyes bore into his. "You need my cock. To spill all this mouthwatering seed."

Alec nodded in agreement before he realized what he was doing.

Miros grinned and let go of his tender nuts to reach again for the basket of soap. Grabbing out a stone, he dunked it in the water. "Bellah." *Good.* "So we agree."

And then he touched that stone to Alec's hole.

Alec froze. Miros mmm'ed, holding him captive in his stare as he lazily circled it around. Again, Alec moaned, this time way too loud. But shit, with as long as his ass had been riding him, any contact there felt frickin' amazing.

"Fuck, Miros. That feels… really fucking good… But honest, I washed there, too." Which was true. He was nothing if not a thorough bather.

Miros slowly shook his head. "You did not wash *here*." The second that last word breached his lips, he pushed the stone into Alec's channel.

Alec tensed at the sting. "Aw, God. What the fuck."

Miros chuckled and reached for a second.

Alec shifted warily. "Two?"

"Tah. Then three."

Again, Alec swallowed, tugging absently at his wrists, as Miros dunked it like the first and repeated. Slow circles—that thankfully also soothed the burn—then a swift press past his sphincter. Alec grunted softly, but didn't attempt to stop him. Not yet at least. After all, Miros was right. He hadn't washed *there.* And in a way, this kinky shit felt pretty good.

Next trip to the basket, Miros grabbed up a fistful.

Alec stared at his hand. "Uh, wow, um, yeah. Just how many does it take to clean an ass?"

Miros stroked Alec's cock with his other hand. "Many." He grinned, starting again. Dip in the water… circle, circle… *push.*

Alec's every muscle spasmed from the fantastical sensation, yet he couldn't help feeling nervous, too. Because even though Miros' playing felt like heaven now, Alec knew that he'd end up in agony. Taken to the brink of rapturous orgasm, only to teeter on the precipice unable to come.

Miros circled and sank another one through. Then a few more after that. Oh, God, that sensual weight behind Alec's asshole. Slowly growing. Filling him up.

The next batch Miros inserted, though, had shit pressing against something sensitive. That swollen spot Alec bumped when finger fucking himself in the river. The spot he'd sensed he better not toy with.

"Oh, God," he groaned, tugging on his binds.

Miros growled and pumped Alec's turgid dick faster. "So arousing it is watching you. So responsive to my touch."

When he sank three more through, Alec flat-out started panting.

"Shit!—Oh shit!—They're pushing against something!—Making me—*Ungh!*—need to come!"

"Yesss," Miros purred. "Your swollen treasure. Soon I will burst it with my cock."

Ah. The "inner jewel" Gesh had spoken about. Alec's prostate. His motherfucking G.

Without warning, Miros wrapped his lips around Alec's crown, then swiftly sank them down his hard shaft.

"Uh! Ah, fuck!" Alec all but shouted. Nothing in the whole world could possibly feel better. And soon nothing would ever feel worse. But no matter how hard Alec's brain shouted *warning!* he just couldn't tell Miros to stop.

Such an alien moment in every way. Never had someone shoved stones up his ass. And never had he been with a male. Human or otherwise. And yet, in this moment he couldn't seem to care.

Miros focused more intently on sucking Alec's cock, evidently done stuffing him with soap. Up and down, up and down, easily taking it all, as his big thumb stroked Alec's ring. Shit, that mouth. That huge, hot tongue. Those stones pressing relentlessly against his G. He couldn't freaking take it. Too many incredible sensations. And yet he didn't ever want them to stop.

Faster the pressure built, getting stronger, till Alec's hips were squirming on that ledge. Abs tensing, toes curling, hole clenching against Miros' finger.

But then Miros pulled Alec's dick from his mouth. "Now," he ordered, back to pumping Alec's shaft. "Release the stones from you *now*."

Too lost in pleasure to question the whys, Alec moaned and gave a push.

Slick, soapy balls emerged in a rush. Alec gasped, then moaned louder. Holy shit. Those rapid little punches tagging his anus were out of this fucking world.

"Again," Miros snarled, pumping him faster. "You make my cock painfully hard."

Why Alec liked the thought of that, he had no frickin' idea. All he knew was that, on top of everything else, Miros' words just set him on fire.

He pushed again with a ragged shout, peppering the water with more stones. Radiating pleasure throughout his channel and junk. Making him shudder and buck.

Miros rumbled in approval and paused from his stroking to suckle Alec's sensitive glans. "Yes. You like how I tend to your body." He thumbed Alec's clenched hole, making it twitch. "Like my pretty stones deep in your ass."

Shit. Forget *like*. Alec fucking *loved* it.

Panting, he nodded, fingers fidgeting above his head. "Yes. Ah, God, Miros. Need to come so bad."

Miros' golden eyes hooded. "I know. And you will. Now, one more time, to release the rest."

Oh, fuck. Just the prospect had Alec's rectum baring down. The last stones left in rapid succession, giving soft kicks as they went. Alec moaned for each one, shivering hard, then slumped as Miros unhanded his cock. Standing, he unhooked Alec's wrists from above and pulled him up on his feet.

"Nenya, Alec." *Come.* "It is almost time to fuck."

Alec whimpered. He wanted to fuck *now*.

Bearings barely in check, he limped out beside Miros, tamping back a stream of strained curses. Because just like he'd feared, Miros' little bit of fun just amped his junk back up to crazy. At least he wasn't alone. Miros' dick was jutting pretty fiercely, too.

The Kríe clutched Alec's nape and guided him forward, graciously letting Alec set the pace. He glanced around. Zaden and Naydo were gone now, too, and—

"You like science?" Finn's husky words interrupted his thoughts. "Tell us, moyos, how do you like *this* experiment?"

Alec turned in the direction he'd last seen the four, then gaped when his eyes found their mark. The twins still had Bailey and Jamis against their fronts with their bound hands still trapped behind their necks. But now they also had them blindfolded, too, with their knees pulled up and tied to their shoulders. Looked like Finn and Filli had gotten resourceful and used the excess rope on the guys' collars. Alec could see it weaved through the crooks of their knees and tied at the base of their napes. Which left them utterly at the mercy of their handlers, whom looked to be having quite the fun.

Alec nearly stumbled as he took in the sight. The twins were gripping their captives' cocks and taking turns plunging them into the other's ass. Damn, they worked really well as a team. The way Filli held Bailey's cheeks spread wide while Finn slid Jamis' dick in and out. And then how Finn swapped and spread Jamis wide while Filli sank Bailey in nice and deep. Those Kríe were one kinky-ass well-oiled machine.

Alec's cock throbbed as he stared. Did the friends even realize they were fucking each other? They were blindfolded, after all, and looked pretty disoriented, squirming in unabashed pleasure.

"You like this research." Filli chuckled. "Feels good. Let us see if we can make you spill."

Their captives groaned louder, anxiously nodding in consent as the Kríe brothers picked up their pace. Faster Filli shoved Bailey's dick through Jamis' ring, using his own hips' driving force.

"Yes! Aw, fuck!" Jamis cried out in bliss.

Bailcy's chest heaved. "Oh, God, yeah! Aw, shit!"

Alec swallowed, heart pounding, unable to believe his eyes. His teammates were absolutely loving it. No way would they want him to intercede.

Miros gripped his arm and pulled him along. "Come. They will join us very soon. The twins' experiment will not succeed."

CHAPTER EIGHT

* * *

They ended up back at compound's heart, where a fresh fire danced in its confines. But now, unlike before, the fire pit was surrounded by huge, hide pillows and lush furs. Piled generously high, they gave the illusion of a great big sea of softness. Blacks, browns, and tans, spotted and striped, the remnants of all the animals they'd slain.

Alec eyed it longingly. After a long day of hiking, it looked beyond amazing. And the perfect place to flat-out collapse. But then he noticed all the Kríe around, too. Wandering about or lounging on plush pillows, eating every shape and color food. Vegetables or fruit, Alec couldn't discern, but suddenly his stomach was roaring.

Miros chuckled and led him to the pack's spread of edibles, gathered abundantly for all to enjoy. Alec grabbed a few items, making sure they weren't fire fruit, then took a huge, juicy bite.

"Mmm. Aw, God. That's really fucking good."

Miros grinned and snagged up a couple things, too, before gesturing to a tall tree nearby. "We climb now."

Alec paused in mid-chew to peer up its looming trunk. "Climb? Why? What about all these great pillows?" He shot Miros what he knew was a pitiful look. "Wouldn't you rather sit on these pillows?"

Again, Miros chuckled and nodded his head. "Yes, but right now they are reserved for the show. We will sprawl out upon them later."

The show? Alec frowned, afraid to even ask.

Miros slipped a satchel strap over his shoulder and filled the bag with his and Alec's food. "Hm." He studied Alec's feet and hands. "No claws. I will have to carry you."

Alec blinked, brows furrowing, as he followed Miros to the tree. "Carry me? Are you serious? Up fifteen fucking feet?"

"Yes. That is nothing. Climb onto my back."

Alec cringed. This wasn't going to feel good at all. Pressing his junk snug against Miros' spine. Already, it was so fucking tender it hurt. But he really wanted to sit down for a second and eat. He was exhausted and food would replenish him.

Sighing in resignation, he mounted Miros' back, wincing and cursing as he went. Miros chuffed in amusement, then began their ascent. And man, did he make it look easy. Alec watched in fascination as the Kríe hoisted them higher, his sharp claws digging effortlessly into the bark. God, he was strong, and in less than a minute had them settling onto a hide-covered platform. Fixed flush against the tree, it faced the pit below, the seat barely a yard wide or deep. Which left few options for where they could sit. Not that Miros was giving Alec the choice.

Propping his spine against the trunk, Miros pulled Alec between his bent knees. "Vai bellah," he rumbled. *Good view.* "Now we eat." He dug into his sack and handed Alec his fruits, then adjusted Alec more comfortably against his chest.

Alec shifted awkwardly as Miros' nipple rings poked his back, but was just too tired and hungry to argue their seating arrangement. Besides, the Kríe was right. They had a pretty sweet view. Kind of like front row balcony seats. But again, he wondered to what kind of show.

Figuring he'd find out soon enough, Alec took the crimson globe and resumed eating. Once more, he moaned in taste bud heaven. "Damn, this tastes like watermelon, but way fricking better. Denser or something. Hardier. Fucking love it." And he honestly did, despite never being a fruit person. But now? He could eat it all day.

Alec paused as something odd occurred to him. Typically, if a human ate too much fruit, it'd give them a wicked case of the runs. But that's pretty much all he and his team had eaten ever since they arrived on this planet. And yet not one time had they had any issues. Not only that but, minus the first day, he hadn't taken any more shits. And having had the same bathroom breaks as the rest of his team, it was easy to conclude that they hadn't, either.

Suspicious, he swallowed his bite of whatever. "Miros?"

"Tah." *Yes.*

"I've got a strange question. Your kind... Do you guys, um... have bowel movements?"

"Bowel movements?" Miros' perplexed tone was downright comical.

"Yeah," Alec chuckled. "The way your body gets rid of waste."

"Ah. I see. Yes, we expel waste from our cocks. Like you and I did together earlier."

Alec stilled with a frown. "Wait. That's the only way? Nothing ever... leaves through your ass?"

Miros grunted in distaste. "*Esh.* Of course not. That passage is for copulation only."

Alec's mouth dropped open. "Get the fuck out."

But before he could venture any further on the subject, Gesh's distant, robust laughter distracted him. Alec glanced to the sleeping quarters across the way, shocked at what he found. Head honcho, pack leader, wrestling playfully atop furs with none other than *Noah* himself.

What. The. Fuck???

Alec blinked, unable to believe it. But sure enough, Noah, blond hair freed from its ponytail, was tussling about *naked* with Gesh. Alec watched in bafflement as the two rolled around, Noah clamoring to straddle Gesh's lean, strong hips, Gesh tossing him into a mound of pelt. They were playing. Fucking *playing.* Like frisky frickin' cubs.

Alec shook his head. He honestly hadn't seen that one coming, either. Sure, he suspected Noah liked Gesh and all, but this took things to a whole new level.

Noah stood, visibly readying to lunge again, and Alec noticed the most telling thing of all. His teammate's dick was only semi-hard. And his nut sac wasn't swollen in the slightest.

Alec's mouth fell open, half shocked, half envious. Noah had gotten laid. Was the only one in their entire unit who no longer needed desperately to come. His features were relaxed, hell the guy was *genuinely smiling*, and best of all, he was still in one piece.

Alec exhaled in relief. He may not know how the two pulled it off, but at least now he knew that they could.

Abruptly, Roni's loud voice rose from below.

"Nenya!" *Come!* "It is time for a feast. One that feeds our eyes and hands, too."

Alec froze. Walking toward the fire pit alongside Roni was a wary-eyed Chet, buck-ass naked. Alec took him in for the first real time. With all those muscles and that huge jutting cock, the guy gave human males a great name. Even his new manscaping job added to his impressive aura.

Unfortunately for Chet, he was bound again, but this time in a whole new way. This time his wrists were up by his head, secured to what looked like a bamboo pole. A bamboo pole that ran across his shoulders and back behind his neck.

Talk about defenseless. Alec tensed even more.

"Móonday," Miros murmured. *Do not fear*. "Roni will not hurt him."

"You sure about that?" Alec watched them approach. "'Cause Chet sure looks like a lamb led to the slaughter."

Miros' deep laugh rushed against Alec's neck. "Trust me. What your friend is about to experience, his body will never want to stop."

Alec's heart pounded anxiously, but from which emotion, he wasn't sure. Fear for his friend? Maybe a little. But something told Alec Chet wasn't really in danger. Which meant excitement was fueling his pulse. Anticipation. And hardcore lust. Because this was the start, he could feel it in his bones, of something that would change him forever. Irrevocably. No rewinds. No ever going back.

He was absolutely confident of another thing, too. A premonition coming from his junk. Before the night was over, regardless of what happened below, Alec would find himself—just as Gesh had predicted—willingly begging for Kríe cock.

* * *

Roni led Chet up onto the lush sea of pelts, then eased him down on his back. Chet settled stiffly, glancing around, but dutifully stayed where he was. Roni grinned down at him, his heated eyes flashing. And even though Chet tried to look calm and collected, it was pretty fucking obvious he wasn't. Skin flushed, chest heaving, hands fisted tight. All telltale signs that he was nervous. Which was totally understandable. Alec would be, too.

But Chet had gotten himself into this mess, even when Alec tried to stop him. Insisting on facing off with a freaking giant, agreeing to Roni's terms of engagement. So now Chet was lying in the bed he made. Fortunately, that bed was *really soft*.

At the far end of the fire pit, a slow, seductive drumbeat rose up and onto the scene. Sensually simple with raw, carnal undertones, like some primitive pulse of testosterone. Alec looked to the males thumping calmly away. Such a weird juxtaposition, their big dangerous claws all but caressing their drum heads. The heat in their eyes, though, looked a lot less docile as they stared like hungry panthers at Chet.

Again, Alec swallowed and tried to relax. Bottom line? Chet was finally going to come. One way or another. Which was good. So as long as Roni didn't maim or kill him, Alec supposed Chet was getting what he asked for. And hell, who knew? Maybe Chet would enjoy it. Love it even, just like Miros said.

Roni dropped to his knees, just as naked at Chet, and wrapped a strip of hide around Chet's eyes. At first, Chet tensed, but then seemed to relax, as if realizing being blindfolded would make things easier. And Alec would have to agree. He had a feeling things were about to get all-out overwhelming.

Roni bent Chet's knee up against his chest and, with another strip of hide, secured it to the pole running across Chet's shoulders. Chet shifted uneasily, mouthing a couple of curses. Roni chuckled and secured his other knee, too, then adjusted them till Chet's thighs were nice and spread.

Alec groaned at how insanely exposed the guy was, his own face heating in sympathy.

Behind him, Miros growled. "It finally begins." Winding his big arm around Alec's waist, Miros tugged him even closer against his chest. "Eat, Alec. Then we will join them, too."

Alec took an anxious bite. Then a few more after that, till his stomach was feeling much better. His other parts, though? Still not so much. But that couldn't be blamed entirely on *senna`sohnsay*. Half was unquestionably due to the spectacle getting started just a few yards below.

Roni started things off with a bit of taste-testing. Specifically, Chet's whole fucking body. The Kríe literally tongued every super-tense inch of him, then suckled his freaking toes. Chet squirmed at that, but otherwise stayed calm. Until Roni sat down in front of Chet's ass and started to stroke Chet's cock. Kind of funny, considering how hung Chet was, that his dick looked so small in Roni's hand.

Chet groaned, lips parting as his hips tried to rock.

Roni's auric eyes hooded. "I am going to share you now." For the first time since he started, the Kríe gestured to his pack. "Come. Enjoy. But do not fuck him. Only I have earned that right."

Chet froze like a statue, as all around, random males joined the fun. Eager lips, hot tongues, and teeth descended. On Chet's neck, mouth, and earlobes. On his thick pecs and nipples. All along his abs and inner thighs. Nipping and licking, pinching and nibbling. Grazing claws over every inch of flesh. Chet shuddered, body tensing, jaw clenched super tight.

Good God. With all those Kríe, Alec could barely even see him. No joke, there were easily ten freaking males crawling all over Chet's body. Alec's dick throbbed painfully, just imagining the feeling. Of that many hot mouths and zealous hands... all at the same fucking time.

Miros let his fruit's empty husk thump to the ground. And then his warm hands slid over Alec's hips and pulled his bent knees closer. Now their legs were propped the same, with Miros' larger ones caging Alec's in.

"I think your friend is happy now." Miros curled one hand around Alec nuts and the other around Alec's cock.

Alec's lashes fluttered. "And, no doubt, anxious to come."

Miros chuckled against his ear, licking its shell. "Oh, he will. For a very long time."

Alec shivered, glancing below as Miros started to stroke. Roni had shoved Chet's hips up and forward and was leisurely tonguing his hole. Another Kríe's mouth was wrapped around Chet's cock, while two others toyed with his nipples. Chet moaned out a stream of more anxious curses.

Alec exhaled and shook his head. There was no freaking way that didn't feel like ecstasy. His backdoor clenched enviously, so needy for contact. Contact like Chet was currently getting.

Roni circled his pointed tongue around Chet's rim, then lapped it from bottom to top. Again and again, making Chet groan. Then more until he clenched and bared down.

Roni chuckled, clearly pleased, and smacked Chet's ass. When Chet barked out a curse, Roni smacked it again. "Quiet, my bitch, and like what I give you, or I will give you what you do not like instead."

Five more times, he spanked each cheek. Chet stifled an oath for each one. With his ass glowing red, and that male still ravaging his cock, Roni smiled and got back to feasting. This time, however, after a good dozen licks, he spread Chet's cheeks and pushed his tongue inside.

Chet's strong hips jerked, but Roni easily held them still as he sank his probe steadily deeper. Alec groaned at the sight, but also at the feel of Miros' hand wrapped around his cock. How it moved up and down with perfect grip as his other hand fondled Alec's balls. Alec shifted, feeling Miros' own erection against his spine, the big fucker reaching between his shoulder blades. Alec tried not to dwell on that, reminding himself that Noah was still intact.

The sounds of sucking and slurping rose from below, along with happy purrs and Chet's moans. Alec glanced down at his team's hired guard. Yup, still covered in a blanket of moving bodies, dark muscles all bunching and flexing. Chet also had two of Roni's glossy fingers shoved up his red-spanked ass. Alec wondered what the Kríe was using for lube. And then he spotted them, small gel-filled bowls sitting randomly atop the pillows. Ah. His answer. Well, sort of at least. What the stuff actually was, he still had no idea.

Roni pumped his digits in and out, emanating a pleased growl as he played. Chet groaned and panted, his bound hands flexing restlessly, while others nipped and suckled his flesh. Earlobes, nipples, along the crease of his groin. Homing in on every erogenous zone Chet had.

Miros' fingers left Alec's balls to gently stroke his hole. Alec clenched hard and sucked in a breath.

"Mmm." Miros leisurely stroked it some more. "You, moyo, will have to relax."

Alec chuckled humorlessly. "Easier said than done. And have you seen your fingernails lately?"

Miros chuffed against his neck, then lifted a hand to his own mouth. Two swift snips of teeth cutting claws. "There. I have removed all threats of danger. Now you must do your part."

Lowering his hand, Miros delved his declawed fingertips into Alec's discarded fruit. Juicy sounds followed as he scooped out some syrupy pulp. Alec tensed in anticipation, and when Miros reestablished contact, Alec's whole body shuddered like an earthquake.

Miros purred in amusement. "You need touch so badly. Have tormented yourself far too long." Without waiting for a reply, he circle-stroked Alec's hole, then slid his first finger deep inside.

Alec moaned, turning his head, shoving his face into Miros' shoulder. "Ah, God. Yes. Need it. So fucking bad." He rocked his hips restlessly, brows drawn tight. And when Miros relinquished Alec's cock to lift his heavy sac, Alec quickly took his place and started stroking.

In, out, in, out, Miros glided his slick finger, then swapped it out for his middle finger instead. In, out, in, out. Then back to his index. Alec squirmed. Miros growled. Then rotated every time, swapping his plunging fingers in quick succession.

Middle—index—middle—index—middle—index—middle—

Alec panted, grimaced, unleashed a restless groan. So Miros changed his kinky play and sank *both* inside. Pumping slowly, then pumping faster, till Alec straight-up writhed against his body.

Miros nuzzled Alec's head and eased to a stop. "You need more. And deeper. Do not move." Shifting his big body, he rummaged back into his sack and pulled out a large hunting knife. One that had a wicked serrated blade, but also a long, bulky handle. Again, Miros scooped out more thick, fruity nectar and slathered the knife to its hilt.

"Watch your friend, Alec, while I take you for a ride."

Alec shuddered and glanced down, doing as told, as Miros pushed his blade's grip past his ring.

"Unnngh…." Alec moaned, eyes rolling shut.

"No, Alec. See what is happening below. The sight is too exquisite to miss."

Alec struggled for breath as Miros sank even deeper, his handle not much thinner than a dick. A human dick, at least, which seemed pretty fitting, since Roni now was riding that of Chet's. Moving up and down, as if doing partial squats, while he straddled Chet's pinned-back hips. Huskily he thrummed, gripping Chet's shins, his heated eyes watching Chet pant. Alec stared as Chet groaned and tried to rock his pelvis, his veiny shaft repeatedly disappearing. Into Roni's body, again and again, as the big male moved atop him.

"Such a hard little cock." Roni squeezed Chet's shins tighter. "It teases me. Makes me want *more*."

A Kríe moved behind them and shoved Roni forward, plastering him against Chet's chest. Those who'd been sucking and biting Chet's nipples quickly moved to other locations.

"You want more?" The male grinned. "*I* will give you more. Make your fuck more pleasing."

Roni shot him a dark look over his shoulder, but didn't move or order him away.

Alec watched the two Kríe, morbidly curious. What was that new male suggesting?

The Kríe dunked the back of his claw into a dish and gestured for Roni to slide forward. Roni eyed him intently as he eased off Chet's dick. Below him, Chet panted, clearly happy for the breather. But then the other male fisted Chet's crown and motioned for Roni to resume. Roni's lips curved slowly in wicked understanding.

The other male smirked, too, and settled onto his stomach, his rugged face aimed at Chet's ass. Then, with fingers still gripping Chet's glans, he angled Chet's dick forward, not up. Roni kept his chest to Chet's and eased back down, clearly planning to take dick *and* fist. Which quickly proved not so easy an endeavor, even with shit all lubed up. Jaw clenching, Roni growled and pushed back harder as another restless moan breached Chet's lips. Roni's thighs flexed. His back arched. His ass cheeks spread wider. Until finally his ring swallowed both whole. Snarling, Roni shot the other Kríe a harsh look, then got back to vigorously fucking.

Alec gaped, utterly speechless. Roni certainly had *more* now. Not only was that male's wrist more than doubling Chet's girth, but damn, his grip around Chet's crown was undoubtedly making one mean prostate stimulator.

Raw, guttural noises rolled up Roni's throat, the double penetration making him shudder. But then it looked like that fist inside him found Roni's special spot.

Hissing, his hips jerked as he fucked even faster. "Yes, Chet. Yes. You no longer tease me."

The other Kríe grinned and stroked his own cock, then turned and shoved his tongue into Chet's ass. Chet's curse came out strained, and Roni hungrily devoured it, before feverishly working his mouth down Chet's neck.

The two writhed on, shuddering and groaning, but Alec couldn't watch another second. That handle up his rectum, rubbing constantly at his G, was making him too fucking mental. Making his whole body tremble.

Panting fast, he squeezed his throbbing dick. "Come—Gotta come—Miros, please—Make me come."

Miros rumbled against his ear. "Does this mean you want my cock?"

"Yes!" Alec rasped as that grip fucked him faster. "Yes! That means I want your fucking cock!"

"Badly enough to beg for it?"

Pleasure mushroomed in Alec's ass. "*Ungh!* Ah, fuck! Yes, I'm begging, Miros! Please!"

"Mmm," Miros purred. "I like this. Beg more."

More? Motherfucker. Alec's body was reeling. "Please," he panted. "Please, Miros. Please. I need it. Please give me your cock!"

Miros thrummed. "Bellah kai, Alec. Bellah key`kai." *Very good, Alec. Very, very good.*

Withdrawing his knife, Miros set it aside and gathered Alec up in his arms. Alec shuddered at the reprieve. Miros shifted his legs over the edge.

Then shoved them both off the platform.

CHAPTER NINE

* * *

Alec tensed as they dropped to the plush pelt below, grunting when Miros landed in a crouch.

"Fucking hell, Kríe. Could've warned me first."

Miros tossed him on a pillow. "Yes. I could have."

Alec shook his head, then stilled when a rough, breathless snarl resounded nearby to his left. Roni. Eyes closed, teeth bared, hips rocking. Riding his Chet and fellow Kríe sex stick like nobody's fucking business. Alec winced. How could Roni's ass endure that shit? Was the male made of freaking titanium?

Miros settled down beside Alec to watch Roni, too, but soon Roni drew to a stop. Eyes flashing, chest heaving, he grimaced and pulled off, then growled at the other Kríe to leave. Beneath him, Chet slumped with a needy groan. Because, just like Alec, he still hadn't come, his dick just as hard as before.

A heartbeat later, the twins arrived, their blindfolded humans in tow. They tossed Bailey and Jamis onto the pelt, then climbed aboard the "sea of soft," too. The scientists twisted awkwardly, trying to sit up, but evidently the Kríe had other plans. Shoving the humans onto their backs, the brothers swiftly straddled their hips. Then, as if wanting to hold them in place, mounted their captives' cocks and sat. The science duo grunted like the Kríe weighed a ton. And honestly, even though the brothers were somewhat smaller, they probably damn near did.

Palming the humans' pecs, the twins thumbed their nipples and friskily rocked back and forth. Now Alec's teammates weren't grunting, but moaning, with their heads craning back into the pillows. Soon, however, the feisty Kríe turned their focus elsewhere, as if suddenly forgetting the men were even there. Just looked on to Roni with their hips absently grinding, barely sparing the slightest downward glance.

If Alec wasn't so damn horny he'd have fucking laughed. Good thing Baily and Jamis were blindfolded. That kind of thing could wound a poor guy's ego.

Zaden and Naydo appeared a moment later. Looking exceptionally flushed, Z was still fully erect as he made his way over to the spread. Alec shifted atop the pillows as the two settled in, Naydo situating Zaden between his knees like Miros had done. Z looked around tentatively, pausing on the twins, then turned his nervous gaze to Alec. A look of *are we seriously about to do this?* flickered in his dark brown eyes.

Alec exhaled and looked away. Because, yeah, they were. Well, he was at least. And he suspected Bailey and Jamis were, too. He just hoped like hell that after all was said and done, they'd all still be able to walk.

Or run, if the case demanded it.

Still breathing heavy, Roni took them all in, then looked down at Chet and grinned. "Time to show your friends what they have to look forward to."

Guess Roni still wanted him and Chet to start things off.

Chet licked his lips and gave a small nod. Not that that pole would allow more. God, he was a trooper. Alec would give him that. With big-ass, brass fucking balls. But Alec suspected another truth about his hired guard, too. That beneath Chet's blindfold, the guy's steely eyes had already rolled back more times than one could count.

Roni settled onto his heels in front of Chet's ass, stroking himself as he studied Chet's hole. Wet and twitching from that other Kríe's tongue, it still looked entirely too small. Even to Alec, from where he sat yards away. Roni was just too long, too thick. Too big for Chet's tight virgin ass. Alec clenched in nervous expectation. Because Roni still seemed determined to give it a shot.

Dragging a tight fist up his own shaft, Roni squeezed out a thick batch of precum. Just like he'd done the night before with Gesh. Using it for lube, he rose to his knees and nestled his crown snugly against Chet's door. Chet visibly tensed, his Adam's apple bobbing.

"Kerra, kenya, kerra," Roni murmured. "Reesha tay." *Relax, warrior, relax. I will not hurt you.*

Slowly, he pushed forward. Paused. Tried again.

Chet grimaced miserably and shook his head, clearly having wanted it to work. "Fuck. Goddamn it. I can't. You don't fit."

Roni pursed his lips, then barked at a Kríe lounging nearby with a friend. "Get the *tachi* venom. And hurry. I need to fuck."

Alec frowned and looked at Miros. "Did he just say venom? `Cause venom does *not* sound very pleasant."

Miros shrugged. "It is actually very smart. *Tachi* venom comes from a predator here who uses it to render prey helpless."

"You mean, the stuff induces paralysis?"

Miros shook his head. "No. That would take away sensation. This venom simply makes muscles weak." Alec quirked a brow. Miros chuckled softly. "Like your cock when flaccid and not aroused. It is limp but can still feel everything."

"Oh." So the stuff was like a Hulk-strength muscle relaxer. And most likely what Gesh used on Noah.

The Kríe strode back and handed Roni a bowl. He also gave him a hand towel and a short, fat object that looked way too much like a butt plug. One, as it were, that was wrapped in cloth from its tip to the base of its handle.

Roni grunted a thank you, then pointed to his companions. "Get the same for them, and we will also need empty tankards." Dunking the cloth-covered tool into his bowl, he watched as it soaked up the venom. When content it was saturated, he brought it to Chet's hole. "Soon you will be ready, warrior, to take my big cock."

Chet must've bared down to help things along because a second later Roni started pushing it in. Chet grunted and winced, until its bulky two-inch body was entirely gone from sight.

Roni rubbed Chet's cheeks soothingly, then turned to the others. "Miros. Naydo. Filli. Finn. Do as I have done."

Perfectly timed, the Kríe returned with four more bowls of venom.

The twins shoved off their playthings, flipped them over, and yanked them up on all fours. Simultaneous trips to those lube bowls next, and they had the guys ready to go. Bailey and Jamis grunted as the Kríe plugged their holes.

Naydo, however, held Z tighter against his body. "Touch yourself, Zaden, and you will relish the feel." Zaden closed his eyes in restless compliance and tentatively stroked his cock. Naydo nuzzled Z's neck as he lubed him up, then slowly eased the tool into place.

Miros was the last to receive his items. Dropping the stout plug into its venom, he set the bowl down and pushed Alec onto his back. Alec swallowed, tensing up, probably because he'd never had venom up his ass. Unsettling, to say the least. Not that Miros seemed to mind. The Kríe just grinned and shoved Alec's knees up, pinning them against his chest.

"Fuck," Alec breathed. "I can't believe I'm doing this."

Miros chuckled, dipped down, and licked Alec's hole. Then growled and tongued faster when Alec gasped. Alec twitched for each flick. Fuck, that shit felt incredible. Even better than Miros' warm thumb.

Miros suckled him, then probed along his clenching ring. "Mmm. Can still taste the sweet juice of dinner."

Alec's lips twitched as he panted. "You saying I taste good?"

"I am saying you taste *delicious*." Sitting back up, Miros flashed him another grin, then lubed Alec's hole and stuffed it.

"Uh!" Alec grunted, shifting anxiously. God, just the feel of it lodged behind his entrance. He winced uncomfortably. "Shit, Miros. Damn. Why's that fucker so short and fat?"

Miros moved up Alec's body, resting his chest on Alec's shins. "Because the depths of your channel are much more flexible. Only your tight little opening risks damage." He dipped down and licked up the side of Alec's neck. "Besides, if venom were to touch your "G," it would render it ineffectual. No release."

Oh, shit. Yeah, Alec definitely didn't want that.

At the center of their gathering, Roni rumbled deep and rough.

Alec's hooded gaze slid toward the sound. His mind, however, was already half lost to the feel of Miros lapping toward his ear.

Looked like Roni had removed Chet's plug and was wiping away the remnants of venom. Once finished, he traced the pad of his finger around Chet's slackened rim.

"Much better," he purred. "Ah, kensa. So much better."

Inserting his index, he circled it around, widening the circle as he played. Then he slid *both* pointer fingers inside and eased Chet's sphincter apart. Damn. That virgin muscle didn't resist at all.

"Tell me," Roni murmured. "Can you still feel my touch?"

"Yeah," Chet rasped. "Fuck, yeah. I feel everything."

"Good." Roni added his middle fingers, too, and opened Chet even wider. "So pliant now. So supple. Going to fill this hole tight." Further he stretched Chet to the point that, no question, he could easily have taken Roni's girth. Roni growled, eyes flashing as he peered inside. "Your jewel is so full, I can see it from here." But then his stare turned downright wicked.

Alec's eyes shot wide as Roni dunked his hand in lube, then sank the thing straight into Chet's hole.

Holy hell. What the fuck was he doing?

Chet squirmed. "Ah, shit! Ah, God, Roni! Shit!"

Roni chuckled darkly. "Does this hurt?"

"*Ungh!* No! But—"

"Then shut up, bitch. There is something I want to show you."

Chet tamped back a groan, jaw clenching tight.

Roni grinned. "Very good, kensa. Good little bitch."

With his free hand, he reached forward and pulled off Chet's blindfold. Chet blinked, restless eyes locking fast with Roni's. Roni smiled salaciously and twisted his wrist, his hand still buried in Chet's ass.

"Can you feel what I am gripping, Chet? Like a plump juicy ball?"

Chet froze, eyes widening as he anxiously nodded.

"Yes. Of course you can. Sensitive, yes?"

Again, Chet nodded super-fast.

Roni chuckled and gripped Chet's cock with his free hand and gave it a couple firm strokes. His other hand got busy, too, playing inside, if Roni's flexing forearm was any indication. Chet fought back a shout, but the thing escaped anyway as his raised hips started to buck.

Roni thrummed excitedly. "Now watch what happens when I give your juicy ball a squeeze." His forearm flexed again, and just like that, precum rifled immediately from Chet's dick.

Chet jerked with a curse, eyes rolling into his head.

Roni laughed and did it again, watching the stuff shoot high, then aimed things for his own mouth next. Shuddering, Chet watched as Roni triggered another blast, watched as he swallowed the thing whole.

Roni growled and licked his lips. "You are exceptionally tasty."

Chet shuddered beneath him. "Fuck, Roni. Please."

Roni gazed at him heatedly. "You want to come. But tell me, do you also want my cock?"

Chet stilled, lips parting, but no words came out. As if admitting such was just too hard. Which Alec could understand, considering Chet and Roni's dynamic. Archrivals by day, fuck partners by night.

Roni grinned. "You still do not know for sure. Perhaps this will help you decide." His buried hand's forearm constricted. "I have just made a fist inside you, Chet. Now I will rub it against your treasure." He swiveled his thick wrist left and right, then gave it a few shallow pumps.

Chet's mouth dropped open on a full-body quake. "Oh m-m-y God. Oh, s-s-son of a b-b-bitch."

Roni laughed again. "This is what my cock would feel like. Do you know if you want it now?"

Chet shuddered even harder, then nodded like a mad man. "Yes! Oh, f-f-fuck yes! I d-d-definitely want your cock!"

Roni kept his fist moving. "Ask nicely, my bitch. Ask nicely for your big Kríe's thick cock."

"Please!" Chet howled. "Aw fuck, Roni, please! Please let me have your thick cock!"

"Deep in your ass?"

"Yes! Deep in my ass! Fucking me hard till I come!"

Roni purred once more. "Very well. You shall have it. Nira knows you have waited long enough." Pulling his hand free, he smiled at Chet's hole, clearly pleased that it'd stayed nice and open. "So ready for me," he mused, squeezing his fist up his shaft. Fresh lube oozed from the thing's broad head. Roni slicked up and rose back onto his knees. Dark eyes churning, he nudged his cock into place. "I am going to fill every inch of you now, until all that you know is *Roni*."

Chet panted restlessly as Roni pushed inside, his fat crown the first thing to vanish. Then inch after inch of thick, dark shaft, until half a foot was solidly buried. Chet bucked with a gasp. Roni must have reached his G.

Pausing, Roni gripped the backs of Chet's thighs. "Are you alright, kensa? Still too much for my bitch?"

But apparently Chet couldn't answer. Jaw clenched, brows pinched, he shook his head, staring at the massive dick entering him.

Roni's lips quirked. "Bellah." *Good.* "Because here comes the rest."

Steadily his hips sank him deeper into Chet's depths. Seven inches… eight inches… nine inches…. Ten….

Chet panted harder, a grimace forming fast. "Fuck. Aw, fuck. Goddamn it. So big."

Roni withdrew to eight inches and rocked back and forth.

*Eight—nine—eight—nine—*Then a fast slam to twelve.

"Ungh! Aw, FUCK!" Chet shouted in alarm.

"Yesss… So deep," Roni rumbled, starting to thrust. "I own you now, warrior. My pretty little bitch. I own you now inside and out."

Chet's pinned frame shook from head to toe. "J-J-Jesus!" he cried out. "So f-f-fucking full!"

Roni grinned and thrust harder. "You like that."

"Ungh! Fuck!"

Alec's heart pounded wildly as he watched them go, shuddering when Miros grazed him with his fangs. His dick was straining, his nuts were throbbing, and he could feel his ass relaxing around that plug. But two seconds later, the sound of Bailey's shout wrenched his gaze past Chet and Roni.

The twins had both scientists laid out on their sides, facing each other, but with their heads in opposite directions. Aka the age-old position sixty-nine. Filli and Fin were spooned up behind them, holding the teammates' top legs raised. Probably to give their dicks ample room as they shoved the things deeper inside. Bailey and Jamis grimaced and arched their backs, until finally the twins were in to the hilt. But then, instead of going thrust-crazy, they paused and gripped the scientists' bound wrists.

"Need us to move now?" Filli wickedly murmured. "To fuck you in your tight little ass?"

"Yes. Shit, yes," Bailey panted. "Need to come."

"So bad," Jamis strained out. "God, please."

The Kríe swapped smirks, then moved the guys' hands so their fingers pressed against each other's junk.

"These cocks are yours now," Finn started to explain, allowing his brother to finish.

"Keep them in your mouths, and we will keep ours in your ass."

Bailey and Jamis stiffened. The twins grinned and slid off their blindfolds.

"Oh, Jesus," Jamis blurted. "Bailey's dick? Are you serious?"

Bailey groaned. "Oh for shit's fucking sake."

The dark males snickered and nodded in unison, giving their hips lazy pumps. "Yes. We are serious. Want to watch you as we fuck."

The two men moaned, rocking their stuffed asses, then reluctantly gripped the other's boner.

"Ugh. For science," Bailey warily conceded.

"For the sake of education," Jamis muttered.

Huge grins spread across the brothers' features as they steadily sped up their thrusts. "Science and education. Ah, yes. Our favorites."

The teammates coughed laughs around each other's dick.

"You guys are fucking nuts."

And Alec would have to agree. He'd honestly never seen anything so depraved. Miros ground his erection against Alec's stomach and hungrily nipped at his neck. And then his huge claw reached between their bodies and grasped hold of both of their shafts.

Faster, he rocked, clutching them tight. "Cannot wait to hear the sounds you make while my cock moves deep inside you."

"Shit." Alec panted, Miros' hand job making him crazy. "Neither the fuck can I."

Miros chuckled and let go to reach further down. Slowly, he ran his finger around Alec's plug where that venom was working its magic. Loosening Alec up, getting him primed. But instead of pulling it out, Miros slid his finger inside and circled it around the handle's base. "Ah, yes. You are nearly ready to begin." Hungrily, he latched onto Alec's neck and sucked.

But that wasn't what Alec wanted to hear. Beyond sexually frustrated, he turned his head and snagged Miros' earlobe with his teeth. "Can't *nearly ready* be bumped to *right now?*"

Miros shuddered, then chuffed against Alec's skin. "Patience, moyo. Just a moment longer. You do not want to tear."

To their left, Naydo's thick timbre derailed Alec's irritation as the Kríe addressed Alec's second in command. "Close your eyes, Zaden. Think back to the river. Imagine we are finishing what we started..."

Alec's sex-starved gaze took them in. Naydo sat on his heels atop the pelt, while Zaden stood straddling his thighs. Z's eyes were shut and he was stroking his cock, most likely like he'd done in the water. And just like in the water, Naydo's two big fingers were buried around back in Zaden's ass. Slowly, he pumped them as Zaden twitched, all the while lapping at Z's balls. Zaden's breaths turned shallow and his legs started to falter.

Naydo paused and looked up, gripping Z's hips. "Let your knees bend, Zaden. I will not let you fall."

Zaden exhaled roughly, but willingly complied. Carefully, Naydo lowered him down to his cock, then eased Z onto his crown. Zaden moaned, but didn't stop stroking his cock. Nor did he open his eyes. Lower, lower, Naydo sank him down, growling when Z visibly jerked.

"Ah... Your jewel. I can feel it against my cock. So full, Zaden. It is ready to pop."

Zaden groaned and nodded, eyes squeezing tight as Naydo's huge dick drove higher into his body. Before long, the Kríe had him fully impaled, and started to move his hips. "This is what you wanted, Zaden, back in that river... And this is what I wanted to give you."

Zaden nodded faster, his pants quickening, too. "Yes. Yes, I wanted it." He grimaced. "So big."

Naydo grinned and thrust harder. "If we had more days, you would learn to love my great big Kríe cock."

Zaden hissed through clenched teeth. "*Ungh!* Holy fuck. Loving your big Kríe cock *now*." As if needing an anchor, he abandoned his dick and hooked his bound wrists around Naydo's neck.

"Yesss," Naydo purred, wrapping his arms around Z's ribs. Latching his mouth to Zaden's hard nipple, he suckled it as they continued to fuck.

Something Alec *really* needed to be doing now, too.

As if sensing his distress, Miros rumbled and sat back, pulled the plug free and reached for lube. Alec's heart hammered in equal parts need and fear. God, he hoped that venom shit worked. But when multiple slick fingers slid past his hole, he didn't feel a single bite of pain.

"Bellah," Miros murmured. "Very, very good." His smoldering golden eyes locked firmly with Alec's. "Relax and rest your hands above your head."

Not wanting to be the reason for any more delays, Alec nodded and quickly complied. Miros seared his body with a hot, hungry look. Then he grabbed his own dick at its base. Fingers tight, he slid his fist up his shaft till a fat bead of precum emerged. Man, Kríe males made some serious lube. And for some reason, Alec found that hot as shit.

Pinning Alec's knees more securely to his chest, Miros pressed his glossy crown to Alec's hole. "I am going to make your long wait worth it. I am going to make you relish Kríe cock." And that was the only heads up Alec got before Miros shoved his big dick inside.

Alec sucked in a breath, eyes snapping super-wide. "*Uh!* Aw, fuck! Did you give me it all at once?"

Miros laughed robustly and shook his head. "No, funny human. Not even close."

Alec tensed, then groaned as Miros pushed himself deeper. Holy motherfucker. He felt fricking enormous. So much bigger than Alec had imagined. He shifted his hips and tried to adjust. Because while his sphincter was being all laid-back and chill, his channel was beyond overloaded. Miros shoved forward again with a little more fervor, igniting Alec's whole fucking body.

"*Ungh!* Ah, God! You just rammed my G!"

Miros chuckled and braced himself beside Alec's shoulders. "Yes," he growled. "Now I do it again." Rocking his hips backward, he briskly thrust them forward.

"Uh!" Alec cried out, arching hard.

Miros snarled and shoved deeper, as if anxious to fill Alec completely. Alec squirmed beneath him, breathing fast. It was all just so crazy. So fucking surreal. He was getting friggin' plowed by an alien. And not just any alien, but a huge freaking male. With skin of midnight purple, and fangs like a mega-vamp. Not to mention his bad-ass horns, all pierced-up like a bred-for-sex demon.

Alec panted, fists clenching above his head as Miros thrust steadily deeper. God, how many inches were crammed in him now? Miros pulled back, then thrust forward harder than ever, slamming their bodies with a *smack!* Alec's everything locked up, stars littering his vision.

"All of you?" he gasped out.

"All of me," Miros purred.

Alec shivered, swallowing hard, and gave a nod. "Good. Now make me fucking come."

Miros' lips curved wryly. "Hold on, moyo."

But before Alec could ask what to hold on *to*, the Kríe started steadily pounding. Breath punched past Alec's lips, followed by grunts—and a shit ton of other blissed-out sounds. Sounds that couldn't even *begin* to describe just how good Miros' gigantic dick felt. So much mass, Alec could barely stand it, and yet he wouldn't give up an inch.

Miros dipped his head down, hot breaths panting along Alec's neck. Fuck, now the Kríe's locks were brushing Alec's skin, stimulating every nerve ending even more...

A deep-throated moan rose up from his chest. "Miros. Ah, shit, Kríe. Ah, fuck yeah. Don't stop."

But now he truly *did* need something to hold on to. Not thinking, just acting, he lifted his hands and grasped hold of Miros' sleek horns. Every single muscle of the huge male tensed, then fell into a violent shudder.

"Alec," he bit out. "You touch me in a way you do not understand." His hips pistoned faster. "But now that you have, I warn you, human, do not even think to let go."

Alec's eyes went wide. Too fast! Too hard! Each thrust grinding furiously against his G. His mouth dropped open. His head craned back. His tense fingers gripped even tighter.

Miros growled against his ear, sounding out of control. "Need to mark you! Your hands make me need to mark you!"

But ringleader Roni must've had other plans. Because right as Miros bared his fangs to bite Alec's neck, Roni shouted to a group of Kríe nearby.

"Nenya! Tacha! Rhya shay *tai!*" Come! Hurry! Fuck us now!

And apparently they didn't need to be told twice.

Not five seconds later, Miros grunted and fell forward as a huge male mounted him from behind. Chest heaving, nearly crushing Alec under his weight, Miros struggled to lift himself back up. As soon as he did, though, he roared in raw pleasure, coming as he thrust even faster.

Alec's body quaked viciously, then arched up hard. He could literally feel Miros' dick kicking deep inside him, pumping out hot jets of seed.

"Fuck!" Alec cried, the flood igniting his prostate, exploding bliss violently through his channel. Steaming, thick cum rifled from his cock, pelting him and Miros in the chest. Miros shoved the Kríe fucking him roughly away, pulled out, and threw Alec onto his stomach. But only for a second. Then Alec was yanked to all fours. Next thing he knew, he was unloading in a tankard, with Miros back to pounding his ass.

"Uh!" Alec shouted, face falling into the fur. "Uh! Uh, fuck! Uh, fuck!"

But Miros just kept thrusting, just kept fucking away, while Alec just kept filling up that mug. He didn't stop, either. Didn't begin to even relent, until his body was consumed with non-stop shudders. But even then, his nuts and G kept on going, pelting cum steadily into the tankard. Miros downshifted to slow, as if somehow knowing Alec still had a ways to go.

Long minutes later, Alec groaned into the pelt, his brain finally coming back online. To his utter amazement, as his body lay lifeless, his dick was still gently pumping. He could hear each soft spurt as it entered thick liquid. And man, did that canister sound full. He moaned again, shivering for each small release. Because, technically, he still was fucking orgasming.

Behind him, Miros thrummed, one hand stroking Alec's hip while the other lightly squeezed Alec's sac. All the while, thrusting languidly into Alec's body, until no more sound echoed from the tankard. Then, very carefully, he pulled the mug away, withdrew, and eased Alec onto his back.

Big, bright eyes gleamed down at Alec's face. "You look very sated."

Alec's lips curved. "Can't move."

And that was no exaggeration. Not one muscle was willing to work. But he didn't care, not in the slightest. Even when his ass started leaking. Because for the first time in what felt like a fricking eternity, he didn't have the crazed need to come. In fact, he wasn't sure his body had *ever* felt such peace.

Alec half-expected his rose-colored glasses to finally fade. For the spell he was under to wear off. But surprisingly, it didn't. In truth, as he looked at the Kríe who'd just leveled him, he couldn't feel anything but gratitude.

He stilled, brows hiking as he realized what Miros was doing. "Whoa. Holy shit. Are you… drinking my jizz?"

Miros pulled the tankard away from his mouth and happily licked his lips. "I am, and will continue to until every drop is gone."

Alec grimaced in confusion. "But—But *why?*"

"Because not only is your "jizz" exceptionally delicious, but here, on our planet, all seed is revered. If it is not spilled for procreation, then we consider it nourishment, and return it in full to our bodies."

Alec stared at him. "Oh."

Miros smiled and resumed drinking, emitting happy growls with each swallow.

Alec turned his eyes to find the others in similar situations. Unable to help it, he bit back a laugh. Because beside each contentedly sipping Kríe sat an equally baffled-looking human. Where the twins were concerned, though, things looked a bit different, their tankards laying completely untouched. Made Alec wonder if they'd drank straight from the tap. After all, sixty-nine would make the scientists' cocks reachable, as long as each Kríe drank from the other's pet. Bailey and Jamis certainly seemed good with whatever transpired. Flushed and still panting, they laid with eyes closed, their lips curved in clear satiation.

Alec shook his head and glanced back at Zaden. Seemingly over the shock of what Naydo was drinking, he now looked just as boneless as Alec. Naydo, however, sat nestled against Z's side, idly stroking Zaden's hip. Damn. Those two looked way too cozy.

Sliding his gaze to Chet, Alec exhaled with a smile. He'd finally been untied, and with his head on Roni's lap, seemed more than a little bit sated. Of course, Roni looked pretty replete himself, all casually nursing his "drink."

Alec cocked his head as he eyed them. They looked ridiculously chilled together, too. Which almost surprised him, but yeah, not really.

Because where on one hand he'd have expected Chet to bolt from Roni once freed, Alec also suspected that, regardless of how intense, Chet had just experienced the ride of his life. And just as promised, Roni hadn't hurt him. At least not in a way Chet couldn't handle. Hell, by the look of things, Roni hadn't just left Chet unscathed, but utterly fucking satisfied.

God, this was all too bizarre to digest. To have waited so long to find relief, then to finally have done so at the hands of such beasts? Though in fairness, he couldn't really call them beasts. He *could,* however, call them enigmas. Enigmas with mind-bogglingly, contradictive natures. So unrefined, yet so incredibly intelligent. A species that would to take Alec a very long time to fully wrap his brain around.

A sinking feeling settled into his gut. Would he even *get* a long time? What was going to happen to him and his team now? He looked up at the sleeping structure where he last saw Gesh and Noah. He could only see their feet peeking over the edge, but they didn't appear to be moving. Guess they'd fallen asleep. Thing was, Noah's smaller feet were *between* that of Gesh's. And where Gesh's big toes were pointing up, Noah's were pointing down. Which told Alec they weren't just snoozing super close, but that Noah was literally *on top* of Gesh's body.

Alec swallowed and looked away. Would Gesh still go through with selling them tomorrow? Alec couldn't really think of a reason why he'd suddenly change his mind. Maybe because of Noah, sure, but he kind of doubted it. Gesh and his pack just didn't seem the type who settled down with partners and shit. Yeah, Noah was attractive, and fun, and smart. And yeah, Gesh clearly was fond of him. But overall, looking at the bigger picture, Alec suspected that wouldn't be enough.

As Miros finished his night cap and stretched out beside him, Alec turned and met his eyes.

"Miros?"

"Tah."

"Is Gesh really going to sell us?"

Miros held his gaze for an unsettlingly long time, then exhaled a long sober breath. "Do not think about the future." He pulled Alec closer and nuzzled his neck. "Just close your eyes and enjoy your body's peace."

Yeah, his *body's*. Because God fucking knew, there'd be no peace in his *mind* tonight.

CHAPTER TEN

* * *

The next morning came faster than Alec would have liked. Probably because he'd slept like a baby. But after such shitty sleep the night before and two days of exhausting consciousness, he supposed that only made sense. Hell, he'd essentially been edged for twenty-four hours straight while hiking cross-country non-stop. Shit like that'd take its toll on a guy.

So, yeah, he must've been sleeping super deep, because not only did he wake up feeling totally refreshed, but in a completely different location than where he'd crashed. In fact, the only thing that remained the same was the huge Kríe pressed up against him. Different snooze spot, different fur mound, but definitely the same male. And not just any male, but the one who'd fucked Alec's brains out, then given him his body heat to fall asleep to. The same Kríe, as it were, whose soft, snoring breaths were currently tickling Alec's neck.

He glanced around what was presumably Miro's sleeping cubby, impressed that he'd moved Alec without ever waking him. His lips twitched. Maybe all that cum Miros pumped up his ass had built-in sleeping agents. Because he'd certainly pumped a lot. After they'd finished, Alec's ass had kept seeping right up until he'd fallen asleep.

Come to think of it... He shifted, curious to see if he'd stick to anything. Nope. Not stuck. But definitely nice and sore. Not painfully, just enough to make sure that he felt it every single time he moved. Did he mind that that'd prove to be a perpetual reminder of what he'd engaged in last night? Strangely, not really. After all, it'd been one hell of a pleasurable experience. In truth, the very best one of his life.

Besides, the way he saw it, what happened on Nira stayed on Nira, and he was pretty sure his teammates would concur. That shit didn't need to go down in the log books. It was the team's business and the team's business alone. Their impossibly hot—albeit unexpected—kinky little out-of-this-world secret. Because no doubt about it, what they'd done in front of that fire pit was definitely pervier than shit. And fuck if every one of them hadn't absolutely enjoyed it. Reveled in it. Embraced it, even.

Strange how, by the end, none seemed to even care about how it all began. With Gesh tricking them into eating that fruit, then keeping them as his tag-along captives. Maybe because in the end, he'd never hurt them. Never forced them to do anything they weren't ready to do. And honestly, as ridiculous as it sounded even to Alec, at the end of the day, his team hadn't been kept from any crucial matters anyway. They had an entire year to kill before someone came and got them. In fact, realistically speaking, Gesh finding them like he had might have been their saving grace. Their food rations would've only lasted for so long. And while they all were pretty versed on how to live off the land, Alec had no doubt there were way more predators around than just those ornery dragons. Ones that were just as aggressive and hungry, but lurked *below* the trees, on the ground. Among unsuspecting prey like Alec's team. Sure they had guns, but guns used ammo, and their ammo would eventually run out. After that, all it'd take was one determined pack of whatevers to send their expedition downhill *fast*.

Alec's blood chilled at the thought. Because getting eaten—or worse, eaten *alive*—wasn't exactly a happy visual. So, yeah, overall, despite his unorthodox behavior, Gesh's coming along was probably for the best. He'd provided food and water, shelter and protection, knowledge and insight to the land. Who fucking cared if the dude had wanted to screw them. Again, he hadn't forced himself on anyone. Kríe were just intrinsically sexual creatures, a fact that'd been clear from the start. And a fact they'd never once tried to hide. So the pack liked sex, and Alec's species aroused them. Big deal. Who cared. Human males liked sex, too. Lots of it. And all the damn time. So really, they weren't too different after all.

And if Alec was being honest, he'd have to admit that he was kind of glad Gesh put him in that position. Because all it ultimately did was give Alec a valid excuse to finally get some quality action. God knew it'd been way too fucking long. And while, sure, this was tossing things onto a whole new level of fetish—breaching out not only to sex with other males, but with a completely different species, too—Alec just couldn't find it in him to care. He was an explorer, for fuck's sake. Down to his bones. Driven to discover new worlds, new things, which logically involved *experiencing* them, too. Which he'd done last night in fucking spades, and honestly, would love to do again.

He sighed and glanced out of the sleeping unit's opening, where a couple of Kríe were building a fresh fire. After breakfast they'd undoubtedly be on their way again. To Alec's team's "final destination." This "homeland" the Kríe spoke of. What awaited them there? Would they be forced into servitude? Made to do only God knew what? His stomach clenched as he looked at his bound wrists, feeling another powerful urge to run. No doubt, his self-preservation instincts blaring for him to do something. But he was tied up and naked, locked inside a compound. What the flying fuck could he do?

Pray that Gesh would change his mind, and that was pretty much it.

And there it was, come full circle. The big, fat, bottom-line, glaring reason why meeting Gesh had *not* been good. The Kríe who could've been their biggest ally, but instead was choosing to be their biggest foe.

* * *

Fortunately, breakfast lifted Alec's spirits a little. As soon as Miros roused, he fetched Alec's clothes, then brought Alec to the fire pit for food. Most of the others were already gathered, including Noah and Gesh.

Alec had eyed the two hopefully, looking for signs that the Kríe had changed his mind. Sadly, he hadn't found anything encouraging. Unless Gesh hand-feeding Noah as Noah sat on his lap meant something Alec wasn't aware of. Typically, one might say it did, but knowing this pack? Well... Even humans hand-fed their pets. Pets that often times ended up in animal shelters as, for lack of a better word, unwanted.

Way too strong a parallel as far as Alec was concerned.

So, no, it wasn't Gesh and Noah's cute-but-meaningless-fun that had Alec's brain on brighter things. It was the myriad of fruit wedges, stacked high on a skewer, that Miros had cooked over the fire. Holy shit, how they melted like butter in Alec's mouth. There was something about the fruits' denser flesh that made it a kind of meat in itself. Grilled to perfection, their juices didn't just caramelize, but turned almost savory, too.

Alec moaned, chewing blissfully, not thinking about anything else.

Miros sat down beside him. "You like." He smiled.

Alec nodded and smiled back. "I love."

"Good." Miros' big eyes dropped to Alec's lips. "*Esh.* You eat like an animal."

Alec paused, brows lifting. "I... *I do?*"

"Tah." Miros swiped the corner of Alec's mouth, his thumb coming away glossed with syrup. His full lips quirked as he licked it clean. Alec chuckled and shook his head.

Zaden strode over a minute later while Naydo went and parked it by the fire.

"Z. My man. Have you had a kabob? No joke, this shit's straight from the gods."

Zaden chuckled and sat down, holding a tin mug. "Nope. Not yet. But I'm on my second one of these." He showed Alec his drink and smiled wide. "Best cup of joe in the cosmos."

Alec's brows shot up again. "*Coffee? Are you serious?*"

"No," Z laughed, shaking his head. "But in my opinion, way fucking better."

Alec drew in a slow, deep breath through his nose, getting a nice good whiff. "Ah, God. Yeah. Smells like hazelnut."

"Or at least something comparable. Naydo calls its *kahtcha.*"

Alec eyed it longingly, then looked at Miros. Miros grunted and rose to his feet.

Zaden watched as the Kríe went to get Alec some, too. "He's cool. I like him."

Alec looked at his friend. "You saying he gives you good vibes?"

Zaden nodded. "Yeah. I guess. I mean, they all kind of do." His dark eyes slid over to Noah and Gesh. "But just like us, they've got their demons."

"Demons? What do you mean?"

Zaden shrugged. "You know, vices. Things that make them weak. Or affect their better judgement." He tilted his head in Gesh's direction. "His, for example, is greed."

Alec's jaw clenched tight in understanding. Gesh's "demon" was the thing selling them out.

Chet, Bailey and Jamis ambled over, steaming skewers of food in their hands.

"Hey, guys," Bailey greeted, having a seat.

"Morning." Jamis sat down beside him.

Chet, however, joined them with a grunt, gesturing with his chin to Noah. "What the fuck is up with them?" Never one to beat around the bush.

The five peered over at the cozy couple.

"Don't really know." Alec shrugged. "Guess Noah likes him."

"Huh." Chet watched them. "I mean, I knew Noah was into guys, but…"

Bailey chuckled and shook his head. "At this stage in the game, I think one's orientation is pretty relative. If I'm not mistaken, every single one of us came harder than shit last night." He smirked and lifted a challenging brow. "And not one by a fucking female."

They all swapped sheepish looks, glancing this way and that.

Finally, Alec cleared his throat and motioned to Noah and Gesh. "Well, those two obviously have the strongest connection, but unfortunately it's kind of a moot point. As you know, after breakfast, we're heading back out."

His teammates sobered.

Chet murmured in Noah's direction. "Come on, pretty boy. Crank up your magic. Time's ticking and you're our last ace."

* * *

Back on the leash with wrists snugly bound, and rope ever weaved between their legs, Alec and his teammates headed west, led by their bedmates-slash-captors. Talk about a head-fuck of epic proportions. Miros and Naydo, Roni and the twins? They acted like they genuinely liked the team. So against all odds, Alec had let himself hope that maybe the Kríe considered them closer to equals. Not just mere playthings, or merchandise to sell.

But as the pack continued to pull them along, Alec reluctantly accepted he'd been wrong. These males were fundamentally just way too arrogant, set in their arrogant Kríe ways. Only an idiot would believe that after two days and a fuck, these nomads would suddenly change their thinking. Or in the pack's case, their order of operations. Which, as scavengers living off the land, meant selling or trading anything of value.

So it was up to Alec and his team to get themselves out of this mess. These Kríe weren't their allies. They were dubious and cunning antagonists. Living, breathing obstacles amidst the adventure.

Alec forced himself to swallow that pill, as jagged and bitter as it was. And then he forced himself to focus, because it was definitely time to start plotting. Who knew how long they had until they reached the imminent "homeland."

Shoving one of his bound hands into his right pocket, he dug out that shard of rock he'd stowed. The one Naydo hadn't seen him conceal when he'd returned from helping his pack slay those dragons. Discreetly, Alec snapped the thin stone in half and handed a piece to Zaden. No words were spoken as they walked side by side. Both men knew what they needed to do. Too bad Chet was at the front of the line. If they ever got their binds free, any backup would be a plus. Because it wasn't like the other three could offer much help. They were scientists, after all, not soldiers.

As they trudged along, quietly sawing at their ropes, Alec took in the changing landscape. They'd been heading around the mountain Gesh's compound was built into, tromping through more never-ending jungle. But now their path was definitely climbing higher, leaving all that rainforest behind. From what he could see, they were headed through a passage, a raised ravine of sorts between two mountains.

Soon they were completely free of woodland—with no protective tree cover overhead. Alec realized this was the first time since the day they crashed that they didn't have a canopy shielding them from flyers. He eyed the steep sides of the waterless gorge, wondering what other dangers lurked. On Earth, these parts would be crawling with mountain lions. It occurred to him then that while traveling with the Kríe, they'd never once come across other land predators. Only dragons had threatened, and they'd come from the sky.

As if lured by his thoughts, flyers screeched in the distance. Alec's team tensed instantly, grinding to a stop, but their leash holders just grunted and tugged them on.

A couple yards ahead, where Gesh walked beside Noah, the blond scientist nervously spoke up. "Aren't you worried that they're gonna attack us? Shouldn't we seek shelter or something?"

"Mah." *No.* Gesh pointed to several locations above. "Look carefully. Do you see those small, concealed stations?"

Noah nodded. "Yeah, I see them now."

"Our king has hundreds of sentries atop the mountains, ready to protect the region at all costs. Those stations above us, like countless others, are specifically equipped to ward off flyers."

Alec's team peered warily up at the sky, while Gesh's pack barely batted a lash. Evidently, the competence of those sentries preceded them.

"How do they ward them off?" Bailey asked, stumbling into Jamis. Someone needed to watch where he was going.

"Wait and see." Gesh grinned. "I am certain you will like this."

Not two seconds later, the flyers flew into view, a trio of them, just like before. Guess dragons on Nira liked to travel in threes. Alec tensed, their keening cries sending goosebumps down his spine. But just as they twisted, readying to dive, sleek projectiles nailed them in the side. Shrieking, they jerked, then plummeted out of sight somewhere behind the mountain's steep horizon.

"Damn," Chet muttered. "What kind of shots were those?"

Jamis eyed the sky. "Yeah. Didn't see any blood."

"Electric-charged darts," Roni answered, walking over. "Effective and very powerful."

"Electric?" Alec couldn't help sounding surprised. These Kríe were more advanced than he'd thought.

"Tah. Harnessed from the province's windways and waterfalls."

"Of course," Alec murmured. "Kinetic energy."

Roni nodded. "It is useful for many things, including the defense against invaders."

"Invaders?" Chet asked, back to scanning the sky. Having a military background a lot like Alec, it was no wonder civil conflict piqued his interest.

It definitely piqued Alec's. Made him wonder what kind of fighting took place there on Nira.

"Tah." Roni nodded again. "But few get in. All who enter must do so through this passage. Which, as you can see, is quite easy to defend. The rest of the realm is protected by mountains."

"Manned by sentinels," Zaden muttered grimly. "Packing some serious firepower."

"Tah." Roni grinned.

"Which means escaping would be just as hard as getting in."

The Kríe's smirk faded to a solemn frown, clearing understanding Z's meaning. "Tah," he confirmed, glancing briefly at Chet. "Tah. That is correct."

Conversation pretty much died after that. Probably because everyone was thinking the same thing. The team was about to enter a domain that they might never come back out of. Alec looked at Zaden. Zaden held his worried gaze. Then both men got back to sawing.

CHAPTER ELEVEN

* * *

Unfortunately, those damn rocks fell apart before the ropes did. Stupid things only held up for an hour. To be fair, Alec *had* been working his rather furiously. But damn it, they were running out of time. Already he could see the huge gates approaching, the narrow gorge filling with more travelers.

Bailey exhaled loudly a few feet ahead. "Well I guess this is it, Jamis. End of the line."

He looked at his friend. Jamis held his dispirited gaze. But then a smile tugged at Jamis' lips.

"It was really nice knowing you, Bailey. And for what it's worth, your dick felt really good in my ass."

Bailey blinked. Then flushed. Then boyishly grinned. "Yeah, well, your ass felt really good around my dick. And truth be told, you give awesome head."

Fighting back grins, they playfully bumped shoulders, but just as quickly, sobered back up.

"We're gonna get through this, Bailey. Our journey doesn't end here. As long as we manage to stick together, we'll find a way to survive." Jamis gave his friend another small smile. "We're smart like that. Can work the system. Even if things get rough." His eyes slid back to the nearing gates. "Besides, just think about all the shit we'll learn. As long as they're not torturing us or harvesting our parts, this could be an incredible opportunity. To be imbedded so deeply in an alien culture?" He nudged Bailey's shoulder a second time. "Talk about an explorer's wet dream."

Bailey chuckled softly and nodded his head. "Yeah, I know, you big goofy homo. And you're right. We just need to keep all this shit in perspective. *Positive* perspective, if possible."

Jamis smiled at his friend, then resumed scanning their surroundings.

The closer they got to that big ominous entrance, the busier the area became. Mostly with Kríe, but Alec noticed other species, too. The majority weren't as big, though. Closer to human size or smaller. In fact, as far as Alec could tell, Kríe were the biggest species of all. Which pretty much by default gave them a high-ranking presence, as well as an air of superiority. Not just from their size, though, but because this region was unquestionably their domain. Their turf. For every one creature of another sort, there were at least two dozen Kríe.

Alec peered at the massive gates as they readied to pass through them, his heart pounding anxiously in his chest. At ten meters tall, they towered above, stretching across the entire ravine. Easily twenty meters wide, possibly more, and made of what looked like rubbed bronze. Combine all said traits and those big motherfuckers exuded not just majesty, but dominance. That and a shit ton of straight-up testosterone. Raw and unadulterated.

Which made something else occur to Alec. Scanning those around him milling about, his lips parted in baffled realization. There were no females present. Anywhere. At all. As far as the eye could see. And the eye could see pretty damn far, as it were, now that they had entered inside. Almost immediately the narrow walls had cut away, opening to a huge stretch of land. A massive, flat valley that reached for miles around. Alec scanned straight ahead, then left and right. Even glanced back over his shoulder. But he still didn't spot a single female. Unless they looked exactly like the males. Which was possible, but for some reason he sort of doubted it. Were they not allowed to roam freely? Were they considered inferior? Honestly, who knew how things worked in Kríe culture. For all he knew, they were the ones in charge, controlling things from their hidden pedestals.

Oh, whatever. Alec supposed it didn't matter. He had way more pressing matters to worry about. Like where his team was headed from there.

He looked to the huge structure looming in the distance that resembled some high-fantasy castle. But not like Cinderella's. More like Maleficent's. No, despite being well-kept and majestically adorned, he got the impression that this kind of castle had dungeons. And guillotines.

Every muscle tensing, Alec forced his gaze away. His team may be headed straight for that imposing beast, but they weren't at its doorstep yet. He'd keep his mind off the ominously imminent for as long as humanly possible.

Fortunately, there was a hell of a lot to distract him. Everywhere he looked there were countless things to see. Nirans of every shape and color in what looked to be some sort of town market. Tittering, chortling, squabbling as they bartered. Or if Kríe, chuffing and bossing others around. Alec studied the different walks of life, fascinated by their very existence. But boy, did they exist, and in huge fricking numbers. A sea of diversity in every direction, teeming with colorful activity.

And God, the aromas, the aromas from the flea fair were just as eclectic as its patrons. The teal-haired male coming up on Alec's right was selling something that smelled incredible. Kind of reminded him of roasted pork and cranberries. A variant of the fruit he'd had for breakfast? His stomach rumbled. Well, it did for a second. But then he passed a scale-skinned fellow peddling something that reeked of dirty socks.

Alec grimaced and looked away, only to discover that Nirans all around were starting to stare. At first they seemed surprised, then curious, then... *something else*. Alec shifted uneasily, not liking the scrutiny. If he didn't know better, he'd say they were sizing his team up for meals. That, or rigorous fucks. Thing was, he *didn't* really know better, did he. Thinking back, Gesh *had* said he found Alec's species delicious. Alluring even, as the big Kríe put it. Would other Nirans feel the same way, too? Alec grit his teeth and avoided making eye contact. Definitely didn't want to encourage them.

Another half hour of walking passed when he noticed a maroon male to his left. Big and barrel-chested, he had *two* sets of horns, but just as noticeable were his tusks and small snout. Standing outside an open tent, he beckoned the masses to come buy his goods. Body adornments and accessories of every sort, made of different metals and hide. Piercings, arm cuffs, chest straps, belts... Alec studied the items closely as he passed the male's stand, then looked ahead to examine his captors. What do you know, they were wearing similar items. Had they gotten their stuff there? Probably. Would make sense. Oh, who fucking cared.

Certainly not him, when they were suddenly just minutes from that mammoth.

Alec stared at the castle, no longer able to look away. Goddamn, that fucker was enormous. He took it in further, studying its exterior. While it didn't have a mote and drawbridge like medieval strongholds, it *did* have a protective stone wall. And that protective wall *did* have four corner towers built into its white-washed sides. Beyond was the money, though. The huge, central keep, laden with regal, arched openings. Out of nowhere, Alec imagined himself peering out one of the windows. How many people would a fortress like that sleep? A hundred? Two hundred? Maybe even more? Funny thing, though, was how it not only oozed doom, but an inspiring kind of splendor, too. It was gothic. It was grandeur. It was "oh, fuck" and "wow."

Alec exhaled warily as they continued their approach, the regal gate opening without warning. A stream of patrol guards immediately emerged. Alec watched as they passed and headed toward town, decked out in every kind of black. Black arm bracers. Shin guards. Large, protective kilts. Black shoulder armor and straps across their chests. Yet, even without all that garb bulking them up, they still were easily just as big as Gesh. Who, at the moment, was eyeing them coolly as he led Alec's team to their fate.

Alec glared at the Kríe, ire rising with his stress. Right after those flyers had gotten shot down, Gesh left Noah's side and never came back. Like he wasn't just trying to put physical distance between them, but an emotional kind of distance, too. Afraid he might get even more attached? Would certainly explain his adamance to stay on schedule. The less time he spent with Noah, the less besotted he'd ultimately become. Hell, maybe even guilt was starting to mess with him. Another reason for his cold-shoulder behavior.

Alec frowned. Come to think of it, *all* of the Kríe were exhibiting similar behavior. He glowered at their backs. Guess they wanted to make sure they had time to ready their "blind eyes" for "turning." That and to pack their cold friggin' hearts with a whole lot of motherfucking ice.

Bastards.

Even now he couldn't believe Gesh was really going to sell them. And that his pack was just going to stand there and let him. A sigh left his lungs. What was he saying. Of course he could believe it. It just pissed him off that there was nothing he could do about it.

He scowled down at his hands as that damn leash tugged them along, cursing those useless freaking rocks. He'd needed them. They'd been his only hope. Now what the hell was he going to do?

Gesh slowed things to a stop as they reached the dark bronze doors, swapping brief words with the stationed guards. They eyed his "goods," then inclined their heads in consent. Two remained watchful to market activity while two others opened the way. Gesh's pack and Alec's team were led through a courtyard and up to the castle's main entrance. More rubbed bronze, but on a larger scale. Slowly, the two gigantic doors parted, but not for dramatic effect. More like because those twin behemoths weighed a couple gazillion tons. Seriously. They were at least five meters high and definitely a good foot thick.

The guards led them into an expansive front foyer decked out in more goth-esque opulence. Wrought iron chandeliers with pristine white candles, hanging low from tall, vaulted ceilings. Kríe statues half-nestled into white-stone walls, each holding a pot of cascading flora. Alec eyed the things, then spotted even more above, peering down like gargoyles from a ledge. Except these weren't grotesque. Not even close. Just elegantly eerie...

Continuing on, they were escorted further back to a gargantuan room Alec assumed was the main hall. It was similarly decorated, but with a bit more oomph, and teeming with a shit ton of merchants. Alec regarded them as they talked, then checked out their wares, gathering that it was broker day at the castle. Evidently the king was a recluse who liked to shop in private. And what a wide range of shopping he must do. The hall smelled of everything from animals and hide, to ironware and woodcrafts, to fruit.

The guards led them over to an open spot.

"The king will be with you soon."

The team glanced around, their expressions beyond bleak.

"Jesus," Zaden muttered. "This is fucking surreal."

Chet's jaw ticked. "We've been reduced to goddamn livestock."

The trio, however, was still fairly distracted, taking in every little detail. But soon Noah's brown eyes made their way back to Gesh. The

Kríe muttered quietly with the males of his pack, none of them looking especially happy. Was their guilt eating holes in them, or were they merely put off by the wait? After all, Gesh liked his tight fucking schedules. That much was painfully clear.

The pack leader's gaze flicked abruptly to Noah. Noah held it till Gesh frowned and looked away. Shoulders drooping, Noah frowned, too, mouthing "fucking coward," then turned back to study the crowd.

"Fuck," Bailey cursed. "I wish I had my smart pad. I'd've taken fifty pictures by now."

Chet narrowed his eyes and shoved over to the pack. "Yeah. When the fuck do we get all our stuff back?"

Gesh curtly looked him over. Roni smirked and crossed his arms. "I told you, my bitch. All your stuff is now ours."

Chet stiffened, then bristled from head to toe. "Like hell it is. That shit's fucking ours. And I'm not your bitch, *bitch*. You're selling me."

An emotion Alec couldn't place fell over Roni's features as Gesh angrily stared Chet down. "It is *not* yours. We appropriated it. It is ours now to keep."

"Fuck you, Gesh," Chet bit out, his face turning red.

Gesh growled. "Hold your tongue, or I vow to Nira that I will muzzle you in front of all present."

Chet leveled him with a lethal glare, but didn't say another word.

Roni sighed and shook his head. "Either way, it does not matter. We did not bring your things along."

Chet stepped in close. "Well then maybe," he muttered, "you should take us back so we can get it before you ditch us."

Roni frowned, gazing down into his angry gray eyes. "I would, little kensa, if I were able. I would like to take you back very much."

Chet pursed his lips in blatant frustration. "Fuck!" he barked, rubbing his skull. "Why not just bend us all over right now? For one final ass fuck without lube."

Roni cocked his head, clearly trying to decipher Chet's meaning.

Chet scowled and cussed again. "Nevermind. Just fucking forget it."

"Chet," Roni rumbled softly.

Chet cut him a scathing look. "Don't fucking talk to me. Like ever."

The guards to their left snapped to rigid attention. "Zercy approaches. Receive your king."

Alec turned in the direction the Kríe were looking and instantly spotted the male. He was headed their way as he spoke with another. His aid, maybe? An advisor? Maybe his second in command. Alec took in the sight of him, instantly captivated. Because even though he was Kríe, the same as Gesh, his air was completely different. Not only was he much more refined and lean—though he still packed a boatload of muscle—but his posture and grooming were impeccable. And man, did his towering frame exude imperialism. Power. Ambition. It rolled off him in waves. Like some otherworldly Julius Caesar.

Which in a way was kind of fitting with his current attire. Alec regarded him further as the Kríe closed in. Clothed in what looked like a midnight green tunic—that reached over halfway down his thighs—he'd topped it off with a black leather belt embellished with black beads and a dagger. Trust issues or something? Maybe he just liked sharp objects.

Like Gesh's pack, he too was highly adorned, his metal biceps and wrist cuffs gleaming. As were the piercings along his ears and horns, and the rings worn on every thumb and finger. What Alec noticed right away, though, were his long black dreadlocks. Not only did the things look satiny smooth, but were riddled with masculine beads. Tiger eyes and opal, or at least something similar, making him look downright exotic. Alec swallowed and dropped his gaze, catching a peek of the Kríe's sandals. Goddamn, even his sleek, black footwear was enamoring, all wound up his muscular calves.

Zercy came to a stop in front of Gesh.

Gesh respectfully inclined his head. "My lord. A pleasure to see you, as always."

"Gesh. How are the jungles?"

"Spacious and unrestrictive. Just the way I like them."

The king smirked. "Never one to reside within our mountains' confines. Although, how the rainforests make you happy I will never understand. So primitive and dark, and…" His words tapered off as he noticed Alec's team. Curiously, he regarded them, studying each one, until his eyes stopped abruptly on Alec. "…and wet."

Alec tensed. Oh, hell. That look couldn't be good.

Gesh grunted. "Wet yields food to fill our bellies."

"True…" Zercy murmured, gaze roaming Alec's body.

"And the tree cover keeps flyers at bay."

"Mm." The king clearly wasn't listening anymore. Pivoting on his heel, he strode Alec's way. "Tell me, scavenger, what is this species you have brought me?"

"A very rare treasure, my lord. Perhaps the very rarest."

Zercy stepped inside Alec's personal space, stared, then touched Alec's jaw. "I do not recognize their kind." Idly, he fingered a lock of Alec's hair. "They must come from extremely distant lands."

"Extremely distant. From a planet called Earth."

The king stilled, then cut his keen eyes to Gesh. "They are not of this world? They are not from Nira's womb?"

Gesh shook his head, avoiding all eye contact with the humans. "Two days ago their aircraft crashed in the jungle."

Zercy blinked in surprise, then looked back at Alec. "Aircraft. Intriguing." He studied Alec's face. "They are very rare indeed."

Alec glanced at Chet and Zaden. They warily frowned back.

The king released Alec's small bit of hair to fondle his earlobe instead. Alec tensed—the unbidden contact making him shiver—and quickly stepped back from Zercy's hold.

Zercy's golden gaze flickered with amusement. "Return to me, pet. I am not done with you yet."

Alec inwardly groaned. Oh, God. Here we go. But he just couldn't get his feet to move. Didn't really matter, though, because the guard standing behind him shoved Alec back into reach.

"Ah. Much better." Zercy smiled, resuming. He ran his hands down the sides of Alec's neck, then squeezed Alec's shoulders and biceps. "Strong," he murmured. "Would make a fine worker." But when he accidentally grazed Alec's skin with his claws, Alec sucked in a quick, sharp breath. The king's lips curved. "Strong… but also sensitive."

"*Very* sensitive," Gesh emphasized. "And very *delicious*."

Zercy paused and lifted a brow. "Delicious, too?" His gaze dropped down to eye Alec's crotch. "I assume you are referring to…"

"I am referring to *everything*."

Alec shot ramrod stiff. Noah visibly deflated. Thing was, Alec suddenly had the strongest impression that Gesh had just done them a favor. As if with just a couple suggestive words he'd ensured their future as in-house pets, as opposed to slaves of hard labor.

Zercy's smoldering gaze spiked to flat-out searing. "I cannot wait to taste."

Alec met his eyes, and was immediately ensnared. And he'd thought Gesh and Miros' gazes were mesmerizing. This Kríe's was ten times more powerful. Alec's heart pounded as he held the dark king's stare. Up close like this, Zercy wasn't merely attractive, but terrifyingly stunning. That exotic, flawless skin. Those perfectly shaped lips, all generously proportioned like the rest of him. With eyes that not only reeled a guy in, but bound him down and held him defenseless. To work over, mind and body, in any way he saw fit. Which Alec sensed wouldn't always necessarily lead to pleasure. Because emanating just beneath Zercy's cordial front was an unmistakable air of danger. Of darkness. Like he wasn't quite right. Like the Kríe was tamping back a world of aggression and anything could set him off.

Zercy slid his hands back up Alec's arms and re-palmed the sides of his neck. Stroking Alec's jaw with his big clawed thumbs, he leaned close and slowly inhaled. His features tightened. "You smell like Gesh's pack. Like one of his Kríe." He stepped back, his expression noticeably less amicable.

Turning to Gesh, he got back to business. "I will pay you double my going price."

"Triple," Gesh countered. The king's eyes narrowed. "But I will give the humans' leader as a gift."

Zercy glanced back at Alec. "I do appreciate gifts." Inclining his head, he turned and started away. "You have yourself a deal, scavenger. My treasurer will bring your coin." He motioned to his guards. "Take them to the holding cell and have someone fetch them baths."

And just like that, His Highness moved on, evidently to begin again with other merchants.

Alec's team tensed in unison as a guard reached for their leash, two more moving in behind them.

"Wait," Gesh spoke up. "Allow us a moment."

The guards eyed Gesh impatiently, but in the end stepped back. Gesh frowned at Noah, then headed over to talk to him. Which gave Alec an opportunity to have words with Miros, too. After all, it truly was now or never. Hail Mary and all that jazz.

Shuffling over, he glared up at the Kríe. "Miros," he bit out. "Don't let him do this. We're not fucking cattle to be sold."

Miros looked at him and sighed. "The king likes you, Alec. He will treat you well."

"I don't want him to treat me well. I wanna get the fuck out of here."

"Just remember," Miros continued, as if Alec hadn't even spoken. "As of late he has been dealing with many hardships, so his temperament at times may be... erratic."

Alec stared at him angrily, then glanced at the king. "Well that's just fucking great. Hand me over to a goddamn head case."

Miros eyed Zercy, too. "As long as you do not try his patience, everything should be fine."

Alec scrubbed his face. "This can't be happening. We can't stay here, Miros. We have families, people who need us." Not entirely true, as he'd lost his parents in a car accident, but the rest of the team probably had loved ones. Besides, he had a sweet job that he didn't want to lose.

"Alec." Miros' timbre was laced with regret. "This is not up to me. I am sorry."

Alec started to tell Miros to shove it up his ass, but the sound of Noah's rising voice distracted him.

"Gesh. Don't do this. Don't fuck me like this."

Alec glanced over in time to see Gesh's jaw clench tight. "Noah. I am giving you to the sovereign king. You will never want for anything again."

"I'll want my fucking freedom. Will he give me that?"

Gesh frowned. "You do not want freedom here. It is far too dangerous. For your kind, it would only bring death."

Noah glowered. "I think that's a little dramatic."

"No." Gesh shook his head. "There are creatures here that would end you in the blink of an eye. Or keep you to torture for sport."

"Didn't seem that dangerous when we were traipsing around with you."

"Because they smell us, fear us. Avoid my kind. But even then, we still go out in numbers."

"Then let us stay with *you*." Noah's eyes turned pleading. "Just until our people come to get us."

"Mah." Gesh shook his head a second time. "Our occupation is precarious. You would be a liability."

"We could stay at your home, then. Out of the way. Help out with chores and shit."

Gesh's face turned grim, as if he'd love just that, but didn't have the faith that it could work. Palming Noah's cheek, he stroked it with his thumb. "Meesha." *Precious one.* "You could be happy here. So much happier than with me."

Noah shoved his hand away. "Don't you dare play that card. That you're selling me for my own good. You're making a fucking profit off us! You don't give a flying fuck if I'm happy!"

The higher his voice rose, the more pained Gesh appeared. "Mah." Again, he shook his head. "You are special. I care. I do." Touching their brows, he cupped Noah's face with both hands. "I did not expect to. It had not been in my plans. If things were different, I vow to you, Noah, I vow I would keep you forever."

Noah clutched Gesh's big wrists, his urgent tone spiking. "Keep me forever *now*, Gesh. Things don't have to be different!"

Without warning, he lurched up and crushed his lips to Gesh's. Gesh froze. Eyes wide, he stared at Noah's closed ones. But he didn't move his hands, and he didn't pull away. Instead, he just stood there as Noah kissed him incessantly, pressing their mouths repeatedly together.

It was passionate. It was affectionate. But most of all, it was desperate. As if the thought of never seeing Gesh again terrified Noah more than being sold.

What was also pretty telling, was the shift in Gesh's demeanor. That subtle softening of his rigid stance. The way his mouth had begun engaging Noah's. Awkward at first, but Gesh caught on pretty fast. Which gave Alec the impression the Kríe hadn't ever kissed before. At least not like that, with a lover. Gesh pulled Noah closer on a low, distressed growl. Holy shit. Alec's pulse picked up speed. Was the pack leader having a change of heart?

The king's guards approached. Time had run out. Alec glanced to Bailey and Jamis, who looked exceptionally stressed. Even the twins beside them exuded anxiety. Not that it kept the Kríe from staying nice and quiet. Guess all the fun last night had them too worn out to speak. Then again, Naydo remained pretty tight-lipped, too. Though in fairness, he did appear exceptionally distraught. The way his sad eyes stayed ever diverted from Zaden's face...

Alec regarded his second in command as Zaden intently scanned their surroundings. Knowing his friend, Zaden was scoping out exit routes. Unfortunately, such knowledge wouldn't do him any good, unless those guards decided to untie them. Which Alec seriously doubted they would. But old habits die hard, and truth be told, Alec had already located them all, too.

He shook his head, disgusted all over again. Had these Kríe no fucking ethics? No moral code at all? Were they seriously okay with human trafficking? Granted, Alec's guys were probably the first humans they'd sold, but Jesus, they'd just shared fucking beds!

He wanted to bellow a stream of foul curses. He wanted to punch them all in the face. But most of all he just wanted to get his men to safety, and rid them of this whole fucking nightmare.

To his right, commotion began to arise. Alec turned, then froze in astonishment. Gesh was shoving the guards away, not letting them anywhere near Noah.

"Do not touch him. I have changed my mind. This one is not for sale."

The guards paused, surprised, as if in all Gesh's transactions, he'd never once rescinded on a deal. Further down the hall, talking with his treasurers, the king stopped and looked their way.

One of the guards hustled over with an update. "My liege. He wishes to repeal a sale."

Zercy frowned and gestured something briefly to his aid, then turned and strode brusquely over. Arriving, he glared at Gesh. "What is this business that delays my affairs? I thought negotiations were over."

Gesh squared his shoulders. "Apologies, Your Fairness. I made a mistake. This golden-haired human is not for sale."

The king regarded Noah, then chuckled coolly. "Mistakes are unfortunate and meant to be learned from." His eyes slid harshly back to Gesh. "The transaction is complete. He is mine now, scavenger. If you want your pet back, you must buy him."

Gesh narrowed his eyes. "As you wish. I will bring you three flyers' worth of fresh meat and hide."

Zercy scoffed crossly. "I do not want flyers. I want slaves. And many. Bring me a score of our northern enemy and we will see about selling you your pet."

"A score?!" Gesh thundered. "For one human?"

The king eyed him darkly, clearly vexed by his outburst. "Yes, you are right. My guards can accrue those. Bring me more humans instead."

Gesh stilled. "More... humans?"

Zercy's gaze moved to Alec. "Yes. That is my price."

"But, my lord, their kind. They are very rare."

"Yes, I remember. Possibly the rarest. Though, for your sake, let us hope there are more."

"Tah," Gesh muttered. "There will be. They are coming."

Noah's eyes shot wide. "You son of a bitch! Don't you fucking dare!"

Alec's heart stopped in his chest as he turned to Noah. "You told him about the others?"

Noah paled, shaking his head. "I didn't—I wasn't—I told him before he tricked us. I told him about our ship... and its beacon."

Alec bit back a curse. For all intents and purposes, they'd just set a trap for their rescuers. All Gesh had to do was wait for their arrival. Hopefully, he'd get bored a couple months down and assume they weren't ever coming.

"Twelve months," Gesh growled, glaring at Zercy. "I will have you more humans in twelve months."

Alec bit back an even bigger curse. Goddamn it. So much for Gesh getting bored. Guess Noah told him about the time frame, too. Hell, knowing Gesh, he'd probably take that beacon and plop the thing down at his crib. Easiest catch ever, you're welcome very much.

Noah winced miserably as the rest of the team groaned.

The king just smirked with a shrug. "Then you will have your pet in twelve months, too."

"Give him to me now, and keep the others as collateral."

Zercy laughed. "The others are hardly collateral." Again, his dark eyes slid back to Alec. "They are mine. Every one of them. Mine and mine alone."

Alec shifted under his scrutiny, heart hammering in his chest. God, that stare. Like Zercy wanted to eat him alive. Starting with Alec's cock as an appetizer. Crazy thing was, despite Alec's unease, he also felt a tingle of anticipation. A kind of dark excitement he couldn't explain. Like the king was luring him. Turning him on. But what the hell? That couldn't be right. Sure, this Kríe could probably rock him like Miros had. But it was different, this feeling. Not like with Miros, where the two of them had just wanted to get off. No, this wasn't what friends with bennies felt like. This was way different. This was more. Ugh. It made no sense. An aftereffect of that plant? All Alec knew was that somehow, someway, Zercy was already under his skin. Rubbing at his hot spots. Making his brain stupid. Why the fuck else would Alec's dick be hardening from just the mere weight of his gaze?

Oh, God. Oh, hell. This was so not good. He did *not* need this kind of complication.

Zercy grinned, then turned and gestured to his guards. "Take them to the bathhouse, and then to Sirus. Tell him to get started. To run every test. I want to know everything there is to know about every single inch of this species. And I do mean everything. Inside and out." He cast Gesh a final condescending look. "I have other matters to attend to. This scavenger makes me late." Turning on his heel, he casually strode off, not sparing another look back.

Alex cringed at the ominous implications of his orders as images of alien probing blitzed his brain. Holy son of a bitch. What the fuck had they gotten themselves into?

"I said do not touch him," Gesh growled to his right as the king's guards once again approached. Of course, they didn't listen. Just continued on task with two assuming control of the leash. "I said do not touch him!" Gesh tried to shove them back, tried to fend them off, but was quickly restrained by more guards. And still he fought them, fangs bared furiously, as Noah was wrenched from his side. "Do not touch him!" he roared. "Let him go! *He is mine!*"

Naturally, his pack bounded into the fray, too, as if they'd long since been chomping at the bit. And maybe they had. They'd certainly looked primed, ready for a formidable fight. And man, did they give one, throwing punches, slashing claws. Tossing heavy Kríe to the ground. Unfortunately, like Gesh, they were quickly outnumbered, swarmed by way more guards than they could handle.

Chet, too, fought valiantly, determined to protect his charge. "Get your paws off us," he barked, shoving and shouldering. Head-butting countless Kríe in the face. "I said lay off, goddamn it! Let go!" But the king's guards swiftly overpowered him, too, even with Z and Alec joining in. Next thing Alec knew, all three of them had been wrenched into unyielding, submissive holds.

He could still hear Gesh bellowing, though, as guards dragged him away. "I will come for you, Noah! I vow it! I will come!"

Alec's chest went cold as Kríe led his team toward an exit. He'd failed his men in every way. Who knew what fate awaited them now. Considering the instructions Zercy gave to that Sirus guy, it certainly wouldn't be rainbows and unicorns. More like exam tables with restraints and scary tools.

Oh, God. Search and Rescue, hurry the hell up. And for the love of all that's holy, don't get captured.

Can't wait for more?
Keep reading for a sneak peek of

ZERCY
THE NIRA CHRONICLES
BOOK 2

Astrum Industries Search & Rescue
Location: Planet Nira of the Siri star system
Heart of the Niran rainforests

"Man, this place is wild. I feel like I'm in the Amazon, but in an alternate dimension... tripping balls."

Garret Scott, first captain of the search and rescue team, lifted his brows as he tromped through knee-high foliage. "You've been to the rainforest, Kegan? And done LSD?"

"Yup and yup," his ginger-haired co-pilot chuckled. "Best and worst days of my life."

"Worst? How come?" Eli piped up a few yards back, the former marine's electro-pulse rifle slung over his shoulder. "You almost get eaten by a three-headed anaconda? No wait, by a kaleidoscope-eyed jaguar."

Kegan chuckled again and looked at their six-foot-three escort. "Nope. Those you can shoot. It was the bugs, man. The bugs. The ants and the spiders. Mosquitos the size of your hand."

"Jesus," Helix grunted, blazing a trail up ahead. He'd never admit it, but he was having a blast. Slashing through gargantuan, low-hanging tree leaves with his machete. Hacking through unruly vegetation.

Like Eli, the dark-skinned ex-marine was one of their unit's two large escorts, there to provide safe passage as they searched. Specifically, for the previous team who'd arrived there one year prior. Six Astrum Industries employees just like themselves, sent in the name of exploration.

Unfortunately, the space station lost contact with said team as soon as their ship entered the planet's stratosphere. Many suspected they'd crashed, with damage explaining the lack in communication. Other suspect magnetic interference.

Of course, Garret was inclined to put his money on the former, considering how his own landing went. The crash left his team with only a distress beacon to call for help—just like the first team's beacon that Garret's men were tracking now.

Paris, their tracker, glanced over his shoulder, his piercing blue eyes half-hidden by loose, black bangs. "I've been to the Amazon twice. Why were you there?"

"My volleyball buddies talked me into it," Kegan answered, stepping over a log. "Learned all kinds of shit. To keep snakes away, we poured salt circles around our tents."

Paris nodded, using a gloved hand to tuck a lock behind his ear. "Tobacco water gets rid of leeches, too. They hate that shit."

Garret grimaced and glanced around, scratching his dirty-blond scruff. His teammates' exchange of fun facts was making him wary. "Monster mosquitos. Snakes. Leeches. Fucking hell. This 'alternate dimension' better not have *any* of that shit."

Sasha coughed a small laugh.

Garret glanced back at their medic. Traipsing along beside ink-covered Eli, the guy's expression did *not* provide comfort. "Please tell me you were laughing at something unrelated."

Sasha smirked and gave a shrug, his light-blond mane brushing his shoulders. "I'm just saying, don't get your hopes up. I hosed you down with that repellent for a reason."

"Great," Garret muttered, reaching down to scratch his shin. Suddenly, he felt itchy all over.

Eli chuckled, shifting his firearm on his shoulder. "Don't worry, Chief. If I see anything crawling up your leg, I'll light that fucker up with my rifle."

Garret laughed. "Soldier, if you relieve me of one of my limbs, you are *fired*."

The escort's wolfish snicker rose up but faded just as fast, lost in the cacophony of the forest; mostly insects, but also a plethora of tree creatures, chirping and squawking and clicking and trilling and chattering their noisy little asses off.

One sound in particular, though, became more apparent than the others. Louder, closer, with an incessant staccato that was disturbingly similar to that of pit vipers. Specifically, the rattlesnake, with its telltale warning rattle. Except, where rattlers gave off a rapid, reedy noise, these jangles were slower—and sounded *heavier*—as if its owners were a more substantial size.

Garret frowned and glanced around. "You guys hearing that?"

Beside him, Kegan nodded, looking just as unsettled.

Up ahead, their tracker stopped. "Yeah. Been keeping tabs on it, actually." Paris peered toward some brush. "I think we're being followed."

"Or hunted." Helix chilled from his hack fest to turn in a circle, his dark eyes keenly searching the vicinity. The rattles grew closer. The marine's gaze narrowed. "Yeah, man. I'm counting at least five."

Paris shook his head. "I hear seven." No one contested. The tracker's wicked hearing was one of his trademarks. That and his uncanny sense of direction.

"Fuck," Garret bit out, reaching for his gun. "So, what you're saying is we got a pack of hungry somethings on our ass?"

"Think so, Chief." Paris nodded.

Awesome. "All right, guys. Weapon up."

Already clutching his rifle, Eli eagerly scanned their surroundings. "Time to raze some jungle to the ground."

Kegan cursed and pulled his hand-held Ruger blaster from his chest holster. "I hate being prey."

Sasha drew his pistol, too. "How 'bout we fire some warning shots. Scare them away if we can." He frowned and peered around. "No need to kill the wildlife unnecessarily."

The ominous sounds came closer. The tree chatter quieted.

Helix glanced up and glowered at their hidden audience. "It ain't unnecessary if they're trying to eat us."

"They're just following their instincts."

Helix shot Sasha a look. "So am I, Doc. The instinct to survive."

The rattles grew louder, more agitated—or maybe excited. Then a few menacing rumbles chimed in, too.

Garret stiffened. "Eli. How 'bout that warning shot, soldier?"

"All right, but if that doesn't deter 'em, I'm gonna have to move straight to introductions."

"Introductions?" Kegan questioned, raising his pistol with both hands.

"Yeah, *me* introducing *them* to the new top of the food chain."

"Fine. Whatever. Just do it," Garret grated. "Before they beat you to the punch."

Eli loosed a volley of electro-pulses into the canopy above, the bodiless bullets sending the tree life to instant turmoil. Winged creatures scattered from their tall, leafy hiding places, others dove to branches in every direction. Even entities in the groundcover up and took off, rustling the dense foliage all around them. Tense moments later, everything went quiet. Garret and his team warily glanced around.

"I don't hear 'em anymore. Think they're gone?" Kegan murmured.

Paris slowly shook his head. "No. I don't think so. Pretty sure I can still hear their—"

A braying roar tore through the silence as a black beast emerged, launching from the brush straight ahead.

"Shit!" Eli barked, spraying the creature with more heat.

It bellowed, rearing abruptly, then dropped back on all fours, appearing somewhat stunned, but mostly just pissed. It bared its fangs, its position no more than a dozen yards away. Garret gaped at its appearance. Alarming, yet striking, its face like a giant king cobra. Its hide looked like a lizard too, but its body looked like a panther—a panther three times bigger than the norm. Yellow slashes covered its scales. Matching spikes ran down its spine. And at the tip of its tail jutted three ten-inch barbs.

Sasha stumbled back as Helix raced over, his monster knife fully sheathed, a rifle like Eli's clutched in his hands. He arrived just in time as two more lunged from the left. With a shout, he blasted the closest with sizzling slugs.

"Fuck!" Garret shouted, unloading on them, too.

Kegan did the same, hollering wildly as he fired.

But more just kept coming, and while the team's barrage threw them off balance, it definitely didn't stop them from advancing. Hell, some were moving too fast to hit at all. Juking and cutting turns faster than any animal Garret had seen, which made predicting their next position all but impossible.

Paris darted to Sasha's side, the pair quickly teaming up, firing their blasters as they stood back-to-back.

The skirmish was deafening; six guns rapidly discharging, their attackers' angry bellows just as loud. Adrenaline slammed Garret's system. His heart pounded riotously. The monsters weren't relenting, barely affected by their firepower, like all their piercing electro-pulses were little BB's. What's more, now the creatures had started tweaking their strategy, making their movements more erratic and hard to track.

"Shit! E-mag's empty!" Kegan scrambled to grab another.

It snapped into place just as Garret's ran out. Paris and Sasha quickly fumbled to reload, too. Helix and Eli just kept blitzing with a vengeance, spraying their foes with a stream of asomatous bullets.

"Goddamnit! How many are there?" Garret kicked back into the fray, firing blast after blast as fast as he could.

"Eight—I think!" Paris shouted.

The beasts lunged, jaws snapping. Some took hits. Some dodged. Some jerked backward or sideways, while as others sprang from multiple directions. Their advance was too fast, their erratic movements disorienting. Even their military escorts were getting rattled.

"Motherfucker!" Eli leapt back, barely avoiding the barbs of a tail. "Their hides are too thick! Our ammo's not piercing 'em! Aim for their fucking eyes and throats!"

The team quickly homed in on their faces.

But then one tore out of the brush, slamming Helix hard in the shoulder. Garret watched him go stumbling as the beast chomped down on his rifle and viciously yanked it out of his hands. The firearm went flying.

Helix snarled and quickly righted himself. "Okay, you son of a bitch. *Now* I'm mad."

Manifesting a pistol in the blink of an eye, he unloaded it with a fury into the beast's skull. The creature went down, but right on its heels, another pack mate lunged for Helix's throat. Way too close to fire upon, he slammed its head with the butt of his gun. It staggered to the side, and that was all the time he needed to juice its brain with raw current at point-blank range.

Garret's second e-mag expired. So did the others', but there wasn't any time left to reload. The pack was too close.

"Run!" Eli bellowed, spraying electro-bullets left and right. "They're not backing down! Go! I'll cover you!"

"*What?* No way!" Garret shouted. They couldn't separate.

"I'll catch up in a minute! Now fucking *RUN!*"

Garret hesitated, brutally torn. Goddamnit, they had to stick together.

"*GO!*" Helix roared, yanking a second gun from its holster. With both arms extended, he promptly went to town, pulling his pistols' triggers in quick succession. Eli was his partner, his right hand, his friend. No surprise that he was staying behind to help.

BLAMBLAMBLAMBLAM!

The ex-marines fired furiously, as Garret and the others took off running.

"This way!" Paris shouted. "Up ahead. I see a path!"

They cut slightly left, tearing through the brush, leaping over downed logs, hurdling bushes. Garret's pulse raced chaotically. He could hear Eli's shouts. The two men were already retreating. Not a good sign. Either they were nearly out of ammo, or they'd quickly become overrun by those creatures. God knew, the pair were viciously outnumbered. Last Garret counted, the black beasts' numbers were more than eight.

A few yards to his right, Kegan wove between trees, while to his left, Sasha dashed like a cat. All graceful and shit, but that was just how he moved. Nearly soundless, while Garret and Kegan crashed like rhinos. Up ahead, with a speed and agility that always floored him, Paris led the way like he knew the place by heart.

The soldiers' shouts got louder.

"Move it! *Move it!*" Eli boomed.

Unfortunately, the four's speed was already maxed out. Those rucksacks they were toting were frickin' *heavy.* Just like Garret's, Kegan and Sasha's bounced on their backs, visibly jarring their balance as they ran.

"Faster!" Helix bellowed.

They'd nearly caught up with them. But how? *How in the fuck?* Garret glanced over his shoulder.

Damn it. *That* was how. Both men had straight-up ditched their packs, and the reason why was alarmingly apparent. The creatures were hot on their asses. If the things weren't injured, they would've already taken the guys out.

"Lose your gear!" Garret shouted, shucking his backpack as he sprinted.

It was an order he hated to give, but what was the alternative? Their stuff wasn't going to do them any good anyway if they wound up inside the bellies of those predators.

The team obeyed immediately, rucksacks dropping fast, everyone instantly picking up speed. As Helix and Eli caught up with them, their unit pulled away, steadily growing the distance between their pursuers.

The beasts' heavy paws pounded in the distance, their angry brays echoing into the treetops. Garret glanced over his shoulder. They'd slowed some but were still coming. Hadn't given up. Goddamnit, they must be *really* hungry. Which was disconcerting as fuck, because how long could his team evade them? They only had so much ammo left on their persons.

The sound of rushing water resounded up ahead, followed by Paris' very unhappy curse. Seconds later, the team caught up to him—but only because he'd stopped.

"What's wrong, Paris?" Garret panted. "Why are you stopping? They're still—*Oh, shit.*" Just past Paris' position, between the trunks of countless trees, he spotted a huge drop off... to a river. AKA a cliff. AKA a dead end.

"Fuck!" Eli barked. "Well, come on, let's go left!"

Paris shook his head anxiously. "We can't. The river curves that way. It'd force us back in the direction of those creatures."

"Then to the right!" Garret ordered. "Come on! We gotta go!"

Again, the team took off running, moving parallel to the river. A heartbeat later, though, two of the beasts intercepted their path. Up in the distance, maybe forty yards away. They bared their cobra fangs. Their yellow lizard eyes glowed.

The men slammed on the brakes and did a rapid one-eighty, then beat feet in the opposite direction. But before they could ever even reach top speed, more predators materialized to block that route as well.

The team pulled up short.

"Son of a bitch!" Garret shouted.

With the river behind them, they stared back into the forest, at the only remaining option left to take. It wasn't as if they could dive off the freaking cliff. The water below could be toxic at best. At worst, teeming with creatures worse than these.

But just as they readied to make a dash for it, a third batch emerged in their final option's path. Pushing through the jungle's dense foliage in the distance, their yellow eyes locked like missiles on the team.

"Shit," Helix bit out. "How much ammo you guys got left?"

"Half an e-mag in each pistol," Garret gritted, watching the creatures.

Kegan nodded. "Same."

Paris and Sasha weren't any better.

Eli glared at the beasts, each batch now thirty yards away, licking their chops as they intently stalked their prey. "One e-mag left, and my pulse-rifle's out. Gotta couple boom dogs, though, itchin' to be used."

Helix nodded. "Me, too." He looked at Garret. "I advise we form a semicircle with guns at the ready. Eli and I'll try one more time to deter 'em."

Simple translation? This was their Hail Mary, and if it didn't work, they'd be fighting with fists and knives.

Garret's heart thumped wildly as he motioned to the others. "Backs to the river, men. Be ready to fire on my mark."

The team fell into position as, on either side, Eli and Helix lobbed their first couple grenades. Unlike the frags of their militant forefathers, these puppies blew in only half of the time. They hit the ground with heavy thumps just a few feet from their targets. The beasts brayed angrily, but just as Garret had hoped, a few of them couldn't resist taking a sniff.

BOOM!—BOOM!—BOOM!

A mushroom of energy exploded, lancing blade-like shards into their hides.

Howls rent the trees. Some dropped. Others scrambled. Ultimately, only three went down and stayed down. The rest just shook it off as if their bells had been rung, then turned their murderous eyes back on the team. Great, now they looked more pissed than ever. Planting their front paws, they threw their heads forward and roared louder than motherfucking shit. Leaves everywhere trembled. Even Garret's ears frickin' rang.

"Goddamnit," he bit out.

This was not going well.

Kegan resituated his grip on his guns. "They're like tanks."

"Yeah," Paris chimed in. "With Kevlar skin."

Simultaneously, the beasts charged.

"Again!" Helix shouted. He and Eli chucked two more. Another round of howls erupted as the frag grenades detonated. But the majority kept coming, even as they bled.

"Fuck me," Eli snarled. "After these, I'm frickin' out."

"So am I," Helix grated. "Make 'em count."

The creatures closed in, only twenty yards away, as the very last boom dogs went airborne. But shit, at the rate those ruggedized bastards were suddenly moving, they were going to gallop past before they blew.

"Fire!" Garret shouted. They needed to slow the fuckers down.

All around him, guns unloaded, bullet pulses flying furiously.

The creatures reared back—

BOOM!—BOOM!—BOOM!

More prehistoric bellows. Now they sounding angrier than ever.

A few more dropped, leaving five to contend with. Five vicious monstrosities and—no ammo. Garret cursed and dropped his pistols as the others did the same, each man tugging free his last-ditch hunting knives.

The beasts snarled menacingly, teeth bared, eyes blazing, and commenced again, barely ten feet away.

Eli widened his stance and leaned forward, glaring. "Protect your throat and head. They're most likely gonna go for one or the other."

Helix nodded and brandished his machete. "Aim for the same. If you lose your knife, punch their snouts as hard as you can, or gouge their eyes. Whatever you do, just *don't* play fucking dead."

"Jesus," Garret muttered, heart thundering in his chest.

"*Hate* being prey," Kegan repeated.

Sasha muttered a bleak curse.

Paris shook his head. "Under most circumstances, I'm a pretty solid optimist. But, yeah, it was really nice knowing you guys."

"Fuck that," Helix grated. "We're not dead yet."

"Damn straight," Eli bit out. He shot his friend a look. "If I'm going down, I'm taking those motherfuckers with me."

The creatures stalked closer, finally caging them in.

Pausing, they crouched as if readying to pounce, their yellow-barbed tails slashing back and forth.

Garret braced, gripping his knife. Time to do or die. To greet his maker or find a way to deny him. Whatever ultimately happened, he just hoped it happened fast, because getting eaten alive did *not* sound fun.

But right as the creatures lunged forward with flashing eyes, another set of bellows tore through the treetops. A different kind of roar though, from a clearly different species. Instantly, dark blurs dropped from branches above, landing with keen precision atop the beasts. Instantly distracted, the creatures went ballistic, furiously trying to buck their attackers off.

Garret gaped, utterly shocked, and watched the crazy scene unfold. Huge, dark purple aborigines had just descended out of nowhere and were now flat-out slicing those creatures apart. Snarling with their knees dug into the animals' backs as they gripped their spikes and rode the things like broncos. With one hand, they held on as, with the other, they slashed throats, their jagged blades already glistening with blood. Again and again, the beasts reared back as thick spurts of blood shot from their jugulars.

The team looked on, each face a mask of awe, until several moments later, the slaughter ended. At the feet of the newcomers, all five creatures laid dead, some of their heads nearly severed from their bodies.

Garret swallowed and took his first good look at their rescuers. A half dozen males packed with outrageous muscle, wearing flaps of long, black hide like tribal loincloths. Black dreads draped their shoulders. Small claws tipped their fingers. Gold-pierced horns curved backward from their temples. Pierced horns, just like their nipples and nasal septums, as well as along their big pointed ears.

Chests heaving, bodies splattered in the blood of their prey, they looked at Garret's team and smugly grinned.

Shit. They had fangs, too. Short but *sharp*.

"Beesha," the largest rumbled.

Co-pilot Kegan chuckled warily. "I really hope that means *hi* and not *you're next.*"

THE NIRA CHRONICLES GLOSSARY

NIRA [**neer**-*uh*] 4th planet of the binary star system, Siri. Smaller than Earth, rotating at half the speed.

CHARACTERS

- HUMAN -

SCIENCE & EXPLORATION TEAM
Alec Hamlin – Pilot and first captain. Light brown hair, blue-green eyes.
Zaden – Co-pilot. Black hair. Dark brown eyes.
Chet – Military escort. Buff, covered in ink. Brown crewcut. Gray eyes.
Noah – Astrobiologist. Shoulder-length sandy-blond hair, brown eyes.
Bailey – Astrobiologist. Curly, dark-brown hair. Hazel eyes.
Jamis – Astrobiologist. Shaggy, dark-brown hair. Green-gray eyes.

SEARCH & RESCUE TEAM
Garret Scott – Pilot and first captain. Dirty blond, blue-gray eyes.
Kegan – Co-pilot. Ginger hair, scruffy five o'clock shadow. Green-gold eyes.
Eli – Military escort. Buff. Brown, spikey crewcut, brown eyes. Covered in tattoos.
Helix – Military escort. Buff. Dark-brown, spikey crewcut, dark-brown eyes. Covered in tattoos.
Paris – Expert tracker. Shoulder-length black hair, blue eyes.
Sasha – Medic. Shoulder-length, light-blond hair, blue eyes.

- KRÍE -

JUNGLE PACK MATES
Gesh [gesh] Pack leader. Noah's lover.
Roni [**roh**-nee] Pack mate, Gesh's 'right-hand.' Chet's sensuous adversary.
Miros [**mir**-dohs] Pack mate. Alec's first-time male lover.

Naydo [**ney**-toh] Pack mate. Zaden's first-time male lover.
Filli & Fin [**fil**-ee] [fin] Twin pack mates. Bailey and Jamis' first-time male lovers.

MÚNRAHKI CASTLE [moon-**rah**-kee]
Zercy [**zur**-cee] King of the Kríe
Sirus [**seer**-*uh* s] Head scientist, physician

NIRAN SPECIES

- INTELLIGENT -

Kríe [kree] Muscle-packed, 7+ ft. midnight-purple indigenes, weighing roughly 350 lbs. with golden eyes, black dreads, pointed ears, black horns, small black claws, and short fat fangs. Arrogant and domineering, originating from the Mighty Realm of the Kríe inside the Múnrahki Mountains.

Oonmaiyos [oon-**mahy**-*oh* s] Lean, athletic 6+ ft. pale, luminescent-skinned water indigenes, weighing roughly 225 lbs. with long sapphire/teal hair, fin-tipped ears, and big dark purple eyes. Playful and curious, originating from the aquatic realm of the Oonmaiyos.

- ANIMAL -

Bellacoy [**bell**-uh-coy] Flyers/ dragons

Tachi [**tah**-chee] Large, black, cobra/jaguar-type predators that hunt the rainforest in packs. Contain venom that reduce their quarry to flaccid prey.

KRÍE LANGUAGE COMPILATION

Aussa – To go
Bayo – Pet
Beesha – Greetings
Bellacoy – Flyers/ dragons
Bellah – Good
Besh – Bad
Bukah – Pleasing
Del`ahtchay – Delicious
Denza – Look
D'ish – Now
Dydum – Large river that leads to The Mighty Realm of the Kríe
Eenta – Smart
En – And
Enday – Pleasure
Esh – Kríe sound of disapproval
Feyah - Cold
Kahtcha – Warm beverage
Kai – Very
Kensa – Warrior
Kerra – Relax
Key'kai – Very, very
Kuntah – Entertaining
Reesa – Water
Mah – No
Mahn – Not
Mahneenta – Stupid
May – Me
Meesha – Precious one
Móonday – Do not fear
Moonsah – More
Móotah – Do not like
Moyos – Creatures
Myah – My
Nenya – Come

Ocha – Other
Ochay – Funny
Óondah – To release/ To spill
Otah – One
Otahtah – One at a time
Reckay – I need
Reesa – Water
Reeka – Give
Reesha – Will not harm
Rhya – To fuck
Senna`sohnsay – Fruit of unrelenting fire
Shawní – Trees/ forest
Shay – Us
Tacha – Quickly/ hurry
Tah – Yes
Tai – Now
Tay – You
Titus – Rocky mountain region northeast of the Mighty Realm of the
        Kríe
Tukah – Hungry
Tuga – To get
Vai – View
Way – All of you

KORA KNIGHT

Born and raised in the Northern Virginia, Kora has always loved to read, but it wasn't until her preteen years that she discovered her deep-seated love for writing. With published literary teachers and play writers in the family tree though, that probably shouldn't have come as a surprise. Starting with her involvement in social book forums, she then tried her hand at literary role playing which, in turn, led to her becoming a fervent online independent writer. Since then, she's endeavored to share with the world her impassioned stories of love, adventure and sensual wonderment, her current and most prominent delight being that of m/m erotic romance.

She has recently finished the second installment of her Nira Chronicles series, Zercy, and will be continuing on with a handful of other projects, including the next Upending Tad spin-off for Breck & Kai.

* * *

For fun insights into her stories and characters, including visual and audio muses, as well as glossaries and deleted scenes, visit her website at:

http://www.koraknight.com

You can also find Kora interacting regularly with readers at these social media sites:

https://www.facebook.com/authorkoraknight/
https://www.instagram.com/koraknight/
https://twitter.com/KoraKnight_Auth
https://koraknight.tumblr.com/

35811754R00078

Printed in Poland
by Amazon Fulfillment
Poland Sp. z o.o., Wrocław